Zen and Sex

By Dermot Davis

Congrats Justin !

DermV.

CONTENTS

1   The Look of Love   1

2   The Come On   14

3   Candid Dates   28

4   I Only Want to be With You   41

5   Never take Your Date to a Party   48

6   How to Drive a Woman Crazy in Bed   66

7   Zen And The Art of Relationship   74

8   A Naked Person Can't Tell Lies   82

9   Do I Look Old And Haggard in The Morning,   90

    Sweetheart?

10 Tantric Sex   108

11 Love is a Drug   114

12 Falling in Love Again   124

13 Hello, Mum   130

14 What Infinity Feels Like   136

15 The Columbus Effect   144

16 The Wedding   151

    About The Author   158

1. THE LOOK OF LOVE

It's a beautiful sunset and I'm walking along the palm tree-lined ocean cliff park in Santa Monica, California. I've been coming here a lot lately and it has become my favorite spot to observe courting couples and photographically capture what I like to call, the look of love. Although we've all observed that moment of magical connection between two lovers at some time or another (and many will claim that they exchange that look with their loved one on a regular basis), in my experience, it's quite rare. A definition does not do it justice (it's a know it when you see it kind of thing) but it's that look when two people gaze into each other's eyes, which says, 'I'm so deeply, joyously in love with you.'

I haven't done an in-depth study, so I can't quote percentages, age group breakdowns or demographics and what-not but suffice it to say, it seems that unwed, courting couples are the least self-conscious in public when it comes to unabashed, soulful eye-staring exchanges (often followed by a passionate or tender kiss or perhaps a little bit of tastefully-censored PDA, public display of affection). Come sunset in Santa Monica, Palisades Park attracts dating couples just like stores attract shoppers in the January sales; so much so, in fact, that a single guy all on his lonesome sticks out enough to warrant suspicion, as in: what on earth is this twenty-four-year old guy doing all alone sitting on a park bench, taking up space and preventing honorable, bona fide courting couples from sitting down to take in a romantic, breathless view of the glorious sunset and the majestic blue-green ocean? This is why I bring my camera with me... everywhere.

In the list (not that I really have a list) of what to bring with you to deflect other people from taking notice of your naked aloneness in a public space known to being frequented primarily by dating couples, a decent camera (not some cheapo, use once, throw-away camera, please) would be number two on the list, after a dog.

Walking a dog is hands down *the* best deflector of singlehood that a lone guy could imagine. In fact, not only does a single guy walking a dog not look lonely, miserable and out of place but he may actually attract attention – positive attention – if the dog is deemed cute enough. Unfortunately, the apartment I share with my roommate does not allow pets but I'm not too bummed about that as, realistically, unless the dog is tiny enough (and hence, automatically excluded as being a "man's dog"), it becomes a problem when you want to take it to other dating couple-heavy locales like bars, restaurants, art galleries or movie theaters where generally they do not allow pets.

So, I'll stick with my Cannon EOS Rebel T3 digital camera with the IS 2, 18-55mm lens which works great for long shots as well as those sweet, close up shots when I really want to capture that glint in those sparkly, love-filled eyes. As a photographer by trade, I do know a trick or two about getting the best angle, lighting and composition for a photo, even when using natural light in the field and whether the subjects are willing or not.

I like to think that what I'm doing is a project or a study of sorts, which to my knowledge, hasn't been explored photographically and then shown or displayed before (yes, a major gallery showing of my work with media fanfare would work wonders for my career and look great on my resume). It has all the elements: human emotion, romance, connection, relationship, joie de vivre, mystery and mystique (better) and many other tags I could slip in which would respond favorably to all the major internet search engines.

What I'd really love, though, is to have one of my photos made into a poster and become as successful and iconic as Alfred Eisenstaedt's 'The Sailor Kiss on V-E Day' which was taken in 1945 in Times Square or better still, Doisneau's 'The Kiss by The Hotel de Ville' which was taken on a street in Paris in 1950. Both of these posters have hung on my walls all through my teens and, well, right up to the present day (though I've no idea what that says about me).

It's probably fair to say that these photos were the inspiration behind why I wanted to become a professional photographer to begin with. At least, maybe in the beginning they were but somewhere along the line (perhaps more as a consequence of adolescent hormones), I decided that professional fashion photographers made shit loads of money and got to sleep with whatever super model they desired. I'm sure I could have gone that way but I never really got the breaks.

Instead, I do print advertisements, real estate, event, portraits, weddings and head shots and anything else not too far beneath my dignity that pays okay. I do all right, not great.

Back at my apartment, I take a look at what I've got on the larger screen of my laptop. I don't like to play around with the images too much, in fact, I prefer them to look as natural as possible. What I'm looking for in the photograph is that magic moment of shared connection between two lovers which melts the heart. Trust me, it's harder than it looks to get it just right. Today, I probably took about a hundred photos all told, hitting up as many as twenty different couples; young, old (some looked like they could be in their forties), ethnic (everyone is ethnically ambiguous in L.A.), tourists, natives and every one in-between.

There is only one or two that I like, where I catch both parties with both their eyes open at the same time and I can see enough of their faces where the light hits them just so. Overall yardstick for each photograph: do they melt my heart? Naw.

I have to wonder about that for a moment because

maybe I'm just getting a bit inured to the look of other people's romantic moments. I'm looking at one photo from today where the caption could easily be: It doesn't get any better than this. Am I a tad jealous? I did feel like that once (and it was only once), with a girl called Roxanne. Not sure if I fell in love with her name first and then the girl or the other way around but fall in love, I did.

I took so many photos of her, it was unreal. I never threw any of them out because I always harbored a secret wish, not even a wish, really, just a notion, I guess, in the back of my mind, that we would get back together again. Not sure of the details but in some distant though not too far-off future, she would come back to me and tell me that her life sucks without me, what was she thinking or some such. I would hesitate before taking her back because I wanted her to truly feel the gravity and enormity of the mistake she had made in the first place. Then we'd live happily ever after. Which is well and truly ironic because guess what I got in the mail today? An invitation…to her wedding.

Okay, so all day I've been trying to wrap my head around this. So far, I've come up with zilch or at the very least the same question I asked when I opened up the prissy, pukey pink, satiny envelope with the ridiculously excessive and aesthetically displeasing embossing: what kind of a woman sends a wedding invitation to the guy she just dumped?

My first thought was: WTF, this can't be happening; we just broke up like, last year some time (I know exactly when it was) because she didn't want to get settled and too serious, we were both young, yada, yada, yada…and now, a few short months after her, 'it's not you, it's me,' going-away speech, she's getting married?

Which led me to my second thought: she must be pregnant. Which led to a whole stream of thoughts ranging from sympathy to serves her gosh darn right! Upon further reflection, I came to the realization that no matter whether she is or is not preggers, either way, she has decided that marriage is the answer to all of her problems and she probably roped in some poor pushover of a guy to give her a rock and half of his condo and retirement plan.

Let's face it, the time of their meeting must have been so friggin' short that they barely know each other's last names. Could easily have been a one night stand, in which case I feel sorry for them both (which makes my secret notion of her coming back to me not so far-fetched, after all). Except now, she'll be tainted with a marriage on her mileage log and may even be saddled with a snotty-nosed kid who gets to play with its real dada every other weekend. Am I going to take her back, then?

The kid could be pretty cool - let's say it's a boy - but then again, what if the kid is handicapped or damaged in some way? Maybe they won't notice it at first but a few weeks after she and I get back together, maybe he'll get diagnosed with some form of palsy or a deformity of some kind. What then? Am I going to bring up someone else's kid who needs twenty-four-seven attention and medical care-giving? I won't be able to change my mind at that stage or I'll be considered a selfish, heartless son of a bitch. Which maybe I am for thinking this way but no way am I going to tell my mind to think only politically correct thoughts just so I can look good to myself.

I hear my roommate, Mike come home from work but I keep doing what I'm doing. Mike and I go so far back that we might as well be brothers; we're so chill with each other, it's almost creepy. He's an outgoing, people person that got a job in sales right out of college. Unfortunately, sales doesn't seem to be his thing; he just seems to get by, squeaking past or just below his quotas and sales targets and just barely manages to keep his job.

Having said that, for some strange reason, this current month has been his best month ever and he's closing every sale in sight. According to him, his success is due to being in a relationship with a woman that he's crazy about, which to my mind is total madness. As every economist will tell you, the business world tends to go in cycles: up, down, up, down. The Dow Jones average doesn't care a fart who anyone is sleeping with, except maybe if it's the president of the United States and even then, the president would have months to lie about it before any major stock indices are remotely affected.

I keep telling him that because he's a positive and upbeat, friendly kinda guy, he would make a great personal coach or motivational speaker but invariably he'll ask me what do I know about the real world and what nine to five jobs are like? Not ever having worked a nine-to-five job in my life, I will reply with some lame-ass comment like, "yeah, it's a jungle out there" and that will be it, end of conversation. I don't think we've had a real conversation about anything important in our lives, ever. Which is probably why we've remained best friends.

"Hey, that's pretty cool," Mike says in lieu of a greeting, as he checks out the photos on my laptop. "That's your love project, yeah?"

"Yeah. Some new ones I took today. They're not great."

"Got your text." Mike quickly says, as if this is what he really wanted to talk about in the first place. "What's your next move?"

He is, of course referring to my text to him about the wedding invitation, which complete with expletives and capitals, it may have looked like I was YELLING with rage. But that was spur of the moment stuff and many hours and a few secret beers later, I can now calmly reflect on the whole thing like the reasoned gentleman that I am.

"My next move? I don't know. What do you think?"

"Well, she obviously wants to rub your face in it." Mike says, sounding like he has given the whole situation some considered thought, probably the only thing he's thought about all day: some new drama, yippee. "What's a girl

6

saying if she sends a wedding invitation to her ex? 'You blew it, I'm happy and I'm in love. You've got nobody and you're miserable. You should never have let me go, you total loser.' She's making a point."

"I shouldn't go?"

"If you don't go, it'll look like it was just too painful for you to show up. Then she wins by default."

"So, I should go?"

"If you go by yourself, then you are a total loser and you'll have to suffer her sickly-sweet, forced, sympathetic smile every time she deigns to look at you during the speeches. 'Oh, you poor thing, you've got nobody to love you. But don't worry, there must be someone out there that's perfect for you. Don't give up hope.' No, you can't go alone dude, don't even think about it."

Knowing exactly where Mike was going with this, I finish off his thought process for him. "The only solution is for me to show up with a drop-dead, gorgeous babe who acts like she's crazy about me."

"Bingo." Mike says with gusto. "Then, *she'll* feel like the total loser."

"Absolutely."

"You're not dating a drop dead, gorgeous chick, are you?" asks Mike, after a timely beat, pointing out the obvious.

"Haven't met any I like," I quip and then turn back to my laptop, not so subtly signaling an end to the conversation.

"You've got three weeks," adds Mike, getting in the last word.

I didn't hear Gloria enter the apartment, so she must have come in with Mike and gone to the bathroom or something because she appears again and, as usual, she drapes herself all over Mike like a lovesick puppy. Gloria spends so much time here that she may as well be a third roommate. She does seem to make Mike happy, though, and

I'm happy for him, even if I don't think that they're well matched, which they're not.

She may be gorgeous, (which, as we know is every man's Achilles heel) but she doesn't have too much going on upstairs, at least not on the same level as Mike and I'm sure, at some point, after all the physical stuff dies down, he's going to notice. He'll then probably feel less fulfilled, like there's something missing and casually bring it up with me, over a beer (in jest, of course), in which case it will then be safe for me to point it out to him (also, in jest).

Until then, I'll keep my opinions to myself and support him through this whole honeymoon phase, hoping it doesn't last longer than my tolerance for sickly-sweet PDA in every room of the house.

"Is Martin coming with us?" she asks Mike as the proximity of her lips nibbles at his ear.

"Yeah, come with us, bro," Mike says, turning to me, with genuine enthusiasm. "It's karaoke night at Frankey's."

As I look at Mike and Gloria I suddenly realize that occasionally *they* share that look of love and maybe I should be taking their photograph… nah, that would be way too weird and besides, most times their intimate public moments are such a turn off that I just have to look away.

Truth be told, I think that Gloria is faking it with Mike. It's like she is totally infatuated with him from morning to night, rubbing her hands and body all over him all of the friggin' time like it was their very next date after they've just had sex for the first time or something, which is not natural.

Maybe somewhere in high school she picked up some tricks that this is how to become popular with boys and maybe swapped notes with the other hot chicks in school, slowly getting her technique down and refining it, ever since.

Because let's face it, that shit works. I mean, us guys love that stuff: a super hot chick with an unbelievable bod, draped all over us, treating us like we were the penultimate masculine deity, turning them on with our mere presence.

Can't personally say I've had much of it myself but I've yet to see a guy turn down a foxy chick just because she treats him like a demi-god.

"Who are the photos?" asks Gloria, seeing the still-displayed photo on my laptop screen.

"Aren't they cool?" enthuses Mike. "The way he catches people just at the right moment?"

"Yeah, but who are they, like, anyone we know?" asks Gloria, totally missing the point.

"Just some couples," I add, hibernating the laptop. "It's a project that I'm working on."

"Tourists are always asking me to take their pictures. Asians, they're always taking pictures, ever notice that?" Even as Gloria is talking, I'm looking at Mike to see what his reaction is: is he squirming inside, like me, or seriously considering her musings? I leave her hanging by not responding and let the silence open it up for Mike to respond.

"Come out for a beer, bro," he asks, looking me straight in the eye. How can I say no? Then I remember the last time I was with them both in a bar, when they were mixing booze and PDAs (the heady mix was like watching cuddling and canoodling on steroids). So I say no.

"How are you going to meet someone if you never go out?" chimes in Gloria.

"What kind of woman is he going to meet in bars?" says Mike, coming to my defense.

"That's where we met, moron."

"Martin has higher standards," jokes Mike.

"Dope," says Gloria, giving him a playing slap on the shoulder.

When they both look at me, I realize that they are still waiting on some kind of response from me. "Who said I want to meet someone? I'm quite happy just the way I am, thank you very much."

"Then why are you taking pictures of all these strange

couples you don't even know?" asks Gloria, who obviously, totally doesn't get it. However, I am in no mood to educate her into the art and sophistication of modern thematic photography.

"I need to make a phone call," I say, excusing myself to get some privacy and enjoy some personal space in my bedroom.

"We're leaving in like, twenty minutes," Mike calls after me, and by his tone, I know that he is letting me know that he is not going to accept any lame excuses from me for crying off the mid-week karaoke crunch at Frankey's. Maybe I will meet someone special, who knows? So, I go change.

As far as sports bars go, Frankey's isn't the worst. Let me rephrase that: I don't like sports bars, in general, but mid-week, Frankey's loses the whole sports bar feel and does a fair job of passing itself off as a cozy neighborhood, hipster bar with softer lights and what sounds like eighties music. It's probably an attempt to attract the ladies, which, judging by the numbers in here tonight, they've succeeded. The karaoke hasn't started yet, thank heavens; I guess people haven't drunk enough yet.

As for meeting someone amazing? Not going to happen. Why? I don't want to be mean and single out Gloria but let's just say that now that she has become a member of the team, well, the dynamic has shifted, if you know what I mean. Instead of being two hunter-gatherer males on the prowl, the three of us sit at a table, off to the side; me, playing the gooseberry to a horny couple that can't keep their hands off of each other (and have no interest in mingling with anybody new, period). The only women I'm going to meet here are the ones who mistake the men's restroom for the ladies' when I'm taking a piss. And how often does that happen?

When me and Mike used to hang out here, you'd never catch us coming midweek for any of the hokey bullshit theme nights: karaoke crush, the open mic

comedy/rap/poetry slam, Brazilian night, Coyote Ugly
Tuesday, Fear Factor Wednesday or the sports trivia quiz
bullshit with complimentary and half-price appetizers.

We'd come on weekend nights when the bar was full of
serious drinkers and hardcore partiers who wouldn't be
caught dead at a mid-week poetry anything. We'd wear our
best and most expensive, coolest shit…and we'd mean
business. We'd sit at the bar because every guy worth his
salt knows that bar seats are *the* best seats in the house for
spotting and attracting talent. And attract them, we would.
Okay, so most of the babes only came to the bar to order a
drink but we could slip in a few zingers and one-liners while
they waited to get served (what's a hot chick like you…,
etc.). Most nights, we killed.

"See anyone you like, Martin?" Gloria asks, scanning
the bar.

"Not yet, Gloria. I'll let you know," I coolly respond.

"There's a hottie," spies Mike.

"The one with the weird hair?" asks Gloria, tracking his
sight line. "You think she's cute?"

"Sure," answers Mike, now sounding uncertain so as
not to incur her wrath.

"She doesn't have any boobs and her ass is too fat,"
comments Gloria with a distinct whiff of 'how dare you
think that someone else in this bar is as cute as I am.' "Do
you think she's cute, Martin?"

"Yep. Cute as a button," I answer, bored already but not
afraid to stick it to her.

"Go ask her to dance," suggests Gloria.

No one is dancing and I think they're playing David
Bowie's, 'Ground Control to Major Tom:' good luck
dancing to that weird little musical oddity.

"No one is dancing, Gloria," Mike says, stating the
obvious, but not adding a duh, which I totally would have.

"I don't hear you offering any great suggestions," says
Gloria, turning her attention back to Mike.

"Maybe he doesn't need any help."

"He's just sitting there. Who's going to come over and talk to him?"

"No one's going to coming over and talk to him. It doesn't work like that," says Mike and only I can hear the sigh of frustration in his voice.

"Yeah, so he needs to get someone up to dance or something," she responds, undefeated.

Okay, so this is getting weird. Don't they care that I'm still here? Are they going to start arguing about who has the best mission impossible strategy for hooking me up with someone cute, as if I even need their help?

"Look," I say, hoping to end the madness, "I came here to have a drink with you two but somehow it's turning into some kind of weird game show where I'm the only contestant. Do you mind?"

"Fine. Stay miserable," says Gloria, sounding miffed.

"Stay miserable?" I ask. Where exactly is she coming from?

"You're love sick and broody," she says, like a doctor giving a diagnosis. Love sick? Seriously? And who the heck uses the word 'broody' anymore: her Amish grandmother? But still, she goes on: "People who don't get touched on a regular basis are depressed and are more likely to die of cancer and stuff. It was on TV."

Oh, boy. When does the karaoke start?

"I can't remember the last time you had sex," she says and then turns to Mike and asks him. "Do you?"

Okay, out of respect to my long-standing friendship to my BFF, Mike, I'm not going to get into it with Gloria. No matter how big a pain in the ass she's being, I've seen too many situations in the past where girlfriends totally messed up best bud friendships. I'm not saying it's a conscious thing on their part but I'm not taking the bait and going down that dark road.

I don't want to lose Mike over some dumb-ass bimbo

who's merely passing through, so I say nothing and just kinda look at Mike with a subtle, WTF, plea-full expression. I don't know what he's thinking and maybe he doesn't want to blow his chance of getting laid tonight but for some reason, he ends up taking Gloria's side.

"You *were* different when you were with Roxanne, Marty," he says, as if he were some kind of objective observer, sharing his neutral opinion.

"I'll be right back," I say matter-of-factly, getting up, like it is the most normal and optimal timing to go to the bathroom. I am so pissed, I don't care to take in their reactions as I leap up.

I don't why Mike had to bring up Roxanne's name like that, and especially in front of Gloria. He has barely mentioned her until now and that was only when we were having a beer together, in some dive bar, where nothing else was going on: no babes to be seen and no sports on TV. And even then, he said her name in a tentative way, as if he was testing the waters to see how I would react; either get depressed and clam up for the rest of the evening or go off on her like I hated her guts; spilling venom all over the place. When I got quiet and switched the topic to something else, he got the message and dropped the subject.

It's such a cliché, having a broken heart. I hate it. Just the mention of her name makes me feel like shit. Worse still, I know the only way to forget her is to fall in love with someone else. Then I'll magically forget about Roxanne. Until the new one breaks my heart and I'm back to where I started. Only the name will have changed. It'll then be Kimberly or something. Maybe the trick is to fall in love with someone new and try to hang on to her long enough until I'm too old to give a shit. But then again, maybe the Buddha was right: pain and suffering are the only true constants in life.

2. THE COME ON

"Make sure we see lots of meat, okay? I want you to make those buns look *really* tasty. I should want to sink my teeth into those buns…like I couldn't help myself. You got it?"

"Gotcha," I respond, as the director of the photo shoot tells me how I need to capture the subjects in front of us. We're trapped in a really hot and stuffy studio in the valley. Sweating, I adjust my lens and move closer to find the best angles and most favorable lighting.

"Okay, baby, give me all you've got," I say in my slickest-tongue-of-the-West voice. "That's it, sweetheart, give it to me, there you go. Lots of meat, that's it, don't be shy, baby, no holding back… sexy buns, give it to me, let's see those sexy buns." I give my best impression of a top fashion photographer. I look around at the small crew to see who, if anybody, finds me amusing (preferably a cute chick). Which they honestly should, because I'm talking to and taking photos of a plate of cheeseburger and fries. I'm taking shots for a fast food chain: a small chain new to L.A.

I do catch one crew guy (probably just a day player) expend a hint of energy on a faint smile but the rest of the gang are professionals who don't have a sense of humor at work and most likely consider such antics to be juvenile and amateurish.

Some gigs can be a long drawn out bore but they don't have to be if only some people would lighten up. Not today, I realize. Looking serious and intent upon impressing whoever hired them for the shoot (most crew are just hired for the duration of a project and then have to look for another job), they ignore me. I don't blame them for trying to appear like all that they want to do is work. Freelancers depend upon repeat gigs and word-of-mouth.

I take it in my stride and frame another shot. There's an art to taking pictures of food; it's not all just point and click. The food must be prepared in a special way; maybe some extra food coloring is added and they definitely spray the fries with some concoction that makes them look like they just came from the fryer. I asked one of the prop guys once what they put in the spray and stuff. All he would say is that it's a trade secret.

The first time I shot food was three years ago and it was for the same people. I was actually pretty proud of my work, especially when I stood in line for lunch at one of their outlets and looked up and saw of all my photos on the brightly lit menu display. They really looked neat.

I actually turned to a cute blonde standing in line behind me and part pride, part come on, I told her that I had taken all of the photographs. She looked at me like I was crazy (crazy that I took them or crazy that I admitted to taking them, I don't know). Without saying a single word or even making some noise in her throat as an acknowledgment, she looked straight past me as if I didn't exist. Embarrassed and feeling humiliated, I similarly pretended that I hadn't spoken but truthfully? that stung. To rub it in, some wise ass behind her (I didn't see him wink to his friend but I'm pretty sure he did) clipped my shoulder to get my attention and then with a serious expression on his face said, "I love your work, man." A-hole.

But you know what? I do love my work. I do take pride in capturing the subject at its best and making the client happy, giving them what they want (most of my work projects, like this gig, are from repeat clients). Whether it is food or babies or a secluded, semi-detached house in the suburbs, to me, this work is a perfect combination of art and commerce. I do what I love *and* it pays the bills.

Ever since I got here, I've been checking out this hot chick, Sandy, I heard one of the crew guys call her name. I've been looking for an opening to make some small talk but she's been working non-stop, multi-tasking like crazy: setting up a conveyer supply of food plate combinations, spraying the food that's been lying around too long, even setting up and adjusting some of the lighting. "We're done with number fifteen, bacon cheeseburger with curly fries," she yells to a young crew guy, who logs it.

Working freelance is cool, I like it, but it means that you don't get to see the same people on a continual basis; it's mostly interacting with new folks for a few hours and then it's on to something or someplace else. So, if you see someone you like, you had better act fast. The problem with acting fast is that they don't know me or have time to get my dry sense of humor, so to someone who doesn't pick up on irony, I risk coming off looking like a total moron. As we pack up, I finally get to say something to Sandy. "Long day, huh?"

"I'm used to long days," says Sandy, not breaking stride as she packs up some gear.

"Want to grab a bite?" I ask, with my best mischievous twinkle of the eyes. "I know this great little burger joint just around the corner. My treat."

I have found, through experience, that if you're going to ask a girl out on a date and if she's hot and maybe a level or two out of your league, you ask them out in a jokey fashion. That way, if they are truly interested, they can say, "Yeah, sure." If they reject you, you then tell them that you were joking. Then they "get it" and smile, maybe loosen up a bit and you can actually come out of it looking kinda cool and interesting.

"Are you serious? We've been spraying burger shit all day. I don't think I'll ever eat a burger for the rest of my life," Sandy says, as if I have just insulted her deeply.

"No, I'm not being serious," I say in my best jokey voice. "It was a joke. Go to a burger joint, after this? Seriously."

"Then, why did you ask?" says Sandy, looking at me

like I'm an idiot. As if she is not even remotely interested in hearing any more of my clever retorts, she picks up a heavy tripod and carries it out of the studio: game over.

So, I'm back in the park and it's a couple of hours shy of sunset. There are a few courting couples around but they're not acting particularly romantic towards each other; the coming splendiferous sunset has yet to work its amorous magic.

A few single women pass me by and I give them each a hopeful smile but instead of a tentative smile of acknowledgement, they mostly act as if they are mentally wondering whether their mace spray is in their purse or they left it back in their car. At least, that's what their expressions look like to me. I guess it's hard being a single gal. With all the come-ons they get, I'm sure they wonder to themselves if guys think that walking, or being out alone, is an open invitation to every single male out there to hit on her: Hey, dudes, I'm outside and I'm alone so go ahead, slugger, give me your best shot.

I sympathize, I do, but, seriously, how does a single guy meet a woman if he doesn't actually meet the female of the species? There's a cute woman right now, sitting on a bench, reading a book. How would I ever meet her? At work? It's three o'clock on a Friday afternoon: does she even have a job? She could be an actress or have any other of myriad L.A. jobs where people never seem to work but they still have the time and the funds to hang out at coffee shops at all times of the day and night.

Maybe I could her at her gym (every hot looking man and woman in L.A. belongs to a fitness center) but if she is a gym member, I'd lay odds she belongs to Curves or some other ladies-only gym where women can work out without being hit on by guys like me. I don't live in her apartment block; I don't hang out with my laptop at her closest Starbucks where she most likely picks up her half milk, half soy, skinny decaf latte with a sprinkle of cinnamon every morning. So, how would I freakin' meet her in a natural, cute-meet, just like in the movies, kinda way? Stop her in the street? Impossible.

But then again, that's how my dad claimed that he met my mother. He had been drinking at the time and he was getting all maudlin' and starting to talk atypically tough. Maybe in his head, he was imagining he was Gary Cooper or Clark Gable or someone similar (he used to watch all their movies).

"It was on a park bench. That's where she was sitting, all alone. She was the most beautiful woman that I had ever seen. What was I going to do? Keep on walking? And forever regret the day that I didn't have the nerve to say something to the most beautiful girl in the world? What was the worst that could have happened? She could have ignored me." Then he gave what I can only describe as a mischievous, movie star smile (which I'd never seen before or since) and added: "But she didn't."

Okay, dad, you're probably looking down on me right now and encouraging me with that very same smile, urging me to give it a go. And I will.

But not yet. First thing I need to do is reconnoiter and decide on the ideal position from which to casually interact. Then I need to work up some courage.

I manage to make it to the railing overlooking the cliff, just a few feet away from where the cute girl with the book sits, oblivious to my plotting. Now all I have to do is sit beside her and engage her in small talk. Of course, I need to look and act as naturally and nonchalantly as I possibly can, which isn't easy when I'm this scared. Us guys don't like to talk about it but I've yet to meet a guy that is not secretly terrified of the cold "come on."

The cold come on is worse than the regular, more commonly experienced come on. The common come on is where you hit on someone that you know or at the very least have seen before. There's some kind of mutual recognition:

maybe it's someone you fancy that works at Starbucks and has come to secretly name you, "Super Big Tipper," in which case, you've broken the ice and a come on is expected. Even if the fancied is in a relationship, she may still feel aggrieved or less desirable, in general, if you don't at least *try* to hit on her.

Another easier (and equally expected) come on is to approach the chick with whom you have been eye-flirting with in a bar. (Just make sure that it is actually you and not your better-looking buddy that she has been directing her come-hither looks toward. Sadly, that has happened to me a few times and although it has usually worked out for Mike and the oh-so flirty one, the best I got out of it was a pat on the head for making the introductions. An atta boy head pat never manages to soothe the embarrassment and humiliation, trust me).

No, the cold come on is a killer: you don't have a history, there's no one to introduce you; you didn't get the all clear to approach with her eyes: you're going in cold. And no pressure, but you've only got one chance - just one line - to break through her defenses.

Admittedly, the majority of guys never use the come on; this is root canal surgery to most males. Those brave enough to enter the fray of the cold come on, usually have only one line. Through trial and error over the years, they've honed and perfected their pickup line until it has a greater than fifty percent chance of success. Then they'll use it, again and again.

Come on lines are harder than you think, 'coz let's face it, they all sound corny: "What's a nice girl like you..?", "Haven't I seen you somewhere before?", "What's that you're drinking?" etc. I've noticed lately that many guys have rejected the really smart ones, the ones that you have to think about or the more obvious pick up lines, like: "If a thousand painters worked for a thousand years, they could not create a work of art as beautiful as you," or "I'm not drunk, I'm just intoxicated by you" (I learned the hard way that this one only works in a bar).

Believe it or not, the most oft-used come on line used by guys these days is so innocuous and on the surface, at least, is so innocent (hence its ingeniousness), that it's not even perceived by the recipient as a come on: "What's your name?"

I use it a lot. If you ask the question innocently enough, you're sure to get a name, even if the rest of the conversation is a wipeout. A few times, I've gotten, "mind your own business," in response (or MYOB, if they think they're being cute). In those cases, it's a win-win situation for you coz now you just dodged a bullet by discovering early on that beauty and bitch sometimes do go hand in hand.

In the cold come on, however, the name question is risky. It may be deemed *way* too forward or you might come off looking desperate, rather than the preferred, desirable "cool." Approaching a woman on a park bench and interrupting her reading to ask her name, I may be perceived as a crazy (I'm too well dressed to be mistaken as homeless and touch wood, I've yet to be maced). So instead, today, I opt for my standby pick up line: "Are you a model?" This particular pickup line has about a thirty percent success rate, but that's mainly at Hollywood parties.

I read somewhere that women know within five seconds whether they like a guy or not so I try not to stress so much about the come on line: in truth, they either like you or they don't. I've used the cheesiest pick up lines on women in the past, like, I don't know, "If I were a stop light, I'd turn red every time you passed by, just so I could stare at you a bit longer," and whereas some women gave me a drop dead look and walk off (in retrospect, fair enough), an equal number thought that I was adorable (my word choice, not theirs) and asked me if I had any more one-liners just like it.

Okay. I'm going in.

As I sit on the bench, close, but not close enough to

scare her off, she breaks from her book long enough to give me a once-over. At this point, I can't tell if it's a look of interest or mere self-protection.

"Mind if I sit here?" I ask.

She smiles (what a smile!) and shakes her head, no, go ahead and sit, it's a free country. As she returns to her book, I nervously blurt out, "I just have to ask... are you a model?"

Again, she shakes her head, no. Then she returns to her book. I really should have read the situation better and pulled out my cell phone to intimate that I didn't just sit down because of her, but rather, I have emails to answer and tweets to send. Instead, I keep babbling like an idiot.

"I'm a photographer and work a lot with models. You could pass for one any day of the week..."

Her completely ignoring me; returning to her book, placing her earphones into her ears and turning up the volume on her iPod has a strange effect upon me. Instead of counting my losses and moving on, I continue to talk to her as if we are having a conversation.

"Want to come to a wedding in three weeks? No? You know what? Forget it. I've changed my mind. We're through. Pack your things and be out before I return home..."

I then get up and casually stroll off. Weird, right? In my defense, it is well known that rejection can cause strange responses in people. Maybe the corny pick up line worked better in my father's day, who knows?

As I get back to the apartment, I notice that the TV is on (a sure sign that Gloria is around). So I avoid being funny and shouting, "honey, I'm home," as I sometimes do when I know only Mike is around. Instead, I walk quietly towards my room. The TV gets my attention as I pass by. Whatever cable channel the set is tuned to is showing an old *Rowen and Martin Laugh-In* sketch where an old woman sitting on a bench is approached by a geriatric male, so old and feeble that he's barely able to walk. So he hits on her.

Old Man: Want to go to a movie?

The Old Woman whacks him with her hand bag, hard. He nearly collapses but manages to stay upright.

Old Man: Want to go back to my place?

Again, the Old Woman whacks him, even harder. She continues to whack him until he falls to the ground. He's too feeble to get up.

Old Man: Want to go to a funeral?

The Old Man dies.

I guess the sketch was meant to be funny but considering where I'm at right now, I find it desperately sad. A foot appears at the end of the sofa and I realize that Mike and Gloria must obviously be snuggled up on it. They mustn't have found the sketch very funny either, as I don't hear either of them laugh. When the foot (I can now see that it belongs to Gloria) is joined by another foot, which twists so that the toes now point downward, I realize that they haven't exactly been paying attention to the TV. When the moaning starts, I quietly and hastily tip-toe to my room.

As I check my email, my eye gravitates to an advertisement: a picture of a really cute woman that definitely has that "look of love," which she is sharing over dinner with her date (all I can see of him is the back of his nicely coiffed head). "You could be making a connection, right now," the headline proclaims. The blinking hypertext link offers an invite to "Get started now" by clicking on "learn more."

I ignore the enticing, yet pathetic ad and search through my emails, which are mostly garbage: people mass forwarding jokes, cute photographs of kittens playing with big dogs, trending YouTube videos and Nigerian scammers looking for investors.

Not one personal email in the bunch; not one of them inquiring about my welfare or sharing something of a personal nature. My eye returns to the warm smile of the model in the ad. I do want someone that gorgeous to look at me like that over dinner, over everything, over anything. She looks like she's in love with that guy, like she really cares for him. I bet that he really feels cherished, having someone like her who obviously adores him entirely. And while I know that it's an advertisement and maybe/probably they're paid actors who just met an hour before the photo was taken...still.

Love like that does exist out there.

I just need to figure out how to find it. One day photo jobs and park benches aren't working out for me and I've got three weeks to find someone seriously hot and adoring, so maybe it is time to get focused and more strategic about fixing my love life. Believing that match-making sites are just for losers, I have never really considered them as a way to meet worthwhile women before. Maybe if I sign up and only approach the drop dead gorgeous ones (all I need is just one to say yes, that they will go to a wedding with me), it will work out. I mean, really, what's the big deal? If they turn out to be someone with some substance and not totally insane, maybe we can even take it past the initial meeting and get serious... but that would be a bonus.

I may have a great eye when it comes to other people's photos but choosing the right photo of myself to use for a dating site, a picture that says all the things that I want it to say (young, hip, good looking, successful, confident, fun, ambitious, sensitive and romantic, working professional and all around, good guy) is a harder task than I could have imagined.

When it comes to filling out my personal profile, writing down all my likes and my strengths and my desires and dreams and what I look for in a mate...makes me feel like giving up. I hate talking about myself and I don't give good interviews. When someone asks me to tell them about myself, I normally just clam up. I don't know why, but to me, when I listen to myself talking about myself... it just sounds so much bullshit. So, half way through telling them what an amazing guy I am, I find that I cannot keep a straight face and I either burst out laughing or die inwardly of embarrassment and humiliation. So, even though I get a good start, it takes me till the next day to finish my profile completely.

I have just sent off a bunch of emails, to some carefully selected, especially attractive women, when Mike walks in the door.

"Yes," he says, while fist-pumping the air. I know exactly what it means.

"You closed the last deal?"

"Top of this month's closer's club! I won a trip for two to Hawaii!"

It's fun to see his excitement. He high fives me and does a Rocky Balboa victory dance.

"That's great, Mike. Congratulations!"

Mike doesn't waste any time getting to the kitchen and taking two of the good beers out of the fridge.

"I can't remember when things were last going so well," Mike says, handing me a beer.

"You deserve it," I say but inwardly I am aware of some mixed feelings. I can't seem to decide if I am happy for him or jealous of him; maybe it's a little bit of both. Naw, in truth, I am mostly jealous, especially when he keeps gloating…

"This is going to sound real soppy, man, but I owe it all to Gloria. Being in love is like… you know the story of Midas? Everything he touches turns to gold, right? When you're in love, that's what happens. Everything just turns out right. And the shit that doesn't? Doesn't matter."

"Kinda like being high all the time," I add.

"Yeah. You know what I'm talking about. Don't you?" he says, as if he's really wondering.

"I've been in love, Mike."

"Oh, yeah. Roxanne. Going to the wedding?"

"I'm still thinking about it."

"Let's hit the bars tonight. We can celebrate my deal and score you a hottie, what do you say?" Instantly, I light up inside. Me and Mike hitting the bars together, just like old times.

"I'm in," I say, "I miss the old days."

"What old days?" Mike asks innocently, which makes me doubt my own memories: am I longing for a past that in my mind, seemed like killer fun but, in reality, and perhaps in Mike's head, was pathetically barren?

In retrospect, we did strike out more times than we hooked up and even though I was having a blast, maybe it wasn't so much fun for Mike?

One scene in particular comes to mind, not because it's in any way spectacular but perhaps because it was common and maybe typifies our nights out together. We were sitting at the bar at our regular hangout, Casey's. It was busy, maybe a Friday night and we were dressed to look cool but not so dressed up that people would think that we were trying to look cool. A hot chick came to order at the bar, the first of the evening, so we hit on her.

"Hey," said Mike, with a breezy smile.

"Hey," the hot chick responded, either not interested or playing hard to get, it was too early to tell.

"Heaven must be missing an angel," said Mike and I think he may have winked at her, partly to let her know that he knew it was a cheesy line but mainly to show that he was trying, anyway. Better to say *something* than nothing at all, right? The hot chick mock puked and not in a friendly way, so I decided that I'd help Mike out.

"If I told you that you had a beautiful body, would you hold it against me?" I said, again in an overtly cheesy way.

"Would you hold it against me if I told you that you had shit for brains?" the hot chick responded, collecting her drinks and leaving. I wasn't quite sure what the logic of her question was and I hesitated too long to deliver a more timely and more clever comeback.

"I'd hold it against you, period," I said as she was departing but what should have been a zinger was delivered too late and too lamely to make any difference. Nevertheless, Mike and I laughed and high-fived each other as if we were the ones coming out on top, which clearly we were not. It was pretty pathetic, actually.

"I miss us partying together," I say to Mike, "we don't do that shit, anymore."

As Mike's cell phone rings, Mike holds up a single finger signaling, hold that thought, and answers his phone with unabashed enthusiasm.

"Hey, sweetheart! Yes! I sure did! Pack your bags for Hawaii, baby!"

I could hear screams of joy from the other end of the phone, as I wait patiently and suck down my beer.

"I'm going out with Martin," Mike then says, giving me a smile and a thumbs up, "have a few brewskis." In expectation of a serious night of drinking, I open the fridge to grab a couple more beers.

"Hold on," I hear Mike say to Gloria. He places his palm on the speaker part of the phone. "Mind if Gloria comes along?" he asks as I hold aloft two freshly opened beers.

"No. Sure. Of course not. That's great," I hear myself say. When he takes one of the beers and turns around, I actually make a horrified face, I don't know why, but it was as if now I was in a sitcom and the audience totally got it and was laughing hysterically at the scene. Except this isn't a situation comedy; it's my life and it isn't that funny.

Okay, there's no need to recap another fiasco night out with Migloria (Mike & Gloria). It will suffice to say that Mike did celebrate with Gloria and I did not score a hottie. I did manage to get nicely drunk without embarrassing myself, at least, I don't think. Unfortunately, I spent too much money and, considering that I've lined up a swad of dates, one for almost every night this week, I really need to pace myself and stick to some kind of budget. I'm going to get me a hot wedding date!

3. CANDID DATES

Tracy, in her profile, says that she's twenty-three and in her online photo, she looks like a raving bombshell. I must have gotten her on a bad day as sitting across from me in the restaurant, she looks older and well, not so hot. She also looks like she didn't change out of her office job duds; she's dressed all conservative and her purse looks more like a briefcase (is it a briefcase?). As soon as we sat down, she took out a notebook and a pen and I'm waiting to see what that's about.

I don't know why I'm so nervous. She really isn't my type, so it's not like I care one way or another whether she likes me or not. Actually, that's not true. I do care about whether or not she likes me and even if she doesn't grow on me or maybe I do grow to like her, either way, I want to be the one to do the rejecting. Some part of me... a large part of me *hates* to be rejected by women. I'm pretty sure most guys feel the same.

"Did you get many responses from your posting?" I ask her, mainly to get the ball rolling but also to do some research as to what to expect from the dating site. I am wondering what the usual response to these kinds of email dating inquiries. I sent out a ton of "introductions" but only got a handful of responses.

"You wouldn't believe the number of candidates," she says, almost wearily.

"Do you mean candid dates or candidates?"

"Oh, that's good. I should write that down," she says. I wasn't trying to be witty but maybe I scored my first bon mots of the evening.

"What's your last name?" she asks.

"You're taking notes?"

"Do you mind?"

"I really don't think I'm going to say anything that memorable. This is a date, not an interview, right?" My delivery is self-deprecating and hopefully, humorous.

"Is there a difference?" she asks, completely deadpan.

"Is there a difference between a date and an interview? Seriously?" I grin at her.

"Think about it. What's the first date all about?" She is totally serious.

"Finding out if there's going to be a second?" She actually frowns.

"I have questions about you. You have questions about me. We go through our life histories, right? Where are you from? Where did you go to school? What music do you like…? Just like an interview. Except, less formal."

"And you want to bring the formal back into dating?"

"This is my seventh first date in like, ten days. I need to keep track of who's who. All right?" she says, kinda huffy.

"Of course." I say, while still thinking what really to say. This isn't working out at all but what am I going to do? Cancel dinner? Nothing disastrous has happened so far so I still may be in with a shot. Maybe if she's happy with my answers, she'll loosen up a little; we'll get to know each other, have a few too many drinks and end up back at her place?

I shouldn't judge her too soon and besides, her intensity is kind of a turn on. Maybe she's used to having her own way with guys and she just needs to be challenged. If I answer all her questions, like a willing "candidate," how will I make an impression on her?

I wonder what she looks like without the glasses and the regulation office clothes? If she, literally, let her long hair down and tussled it a bit, she would look ten times hotter. I could bet money that she's a raver beneath the sheets.

"How many years of college have you had?" she asks. Oh, please, I groan inside.

"Don't you think that there's more going on, something of greater depth, than just exchanging facts about each other's lives?"

"Such as?"

"Well, the stuff you can't quantify...the chemistry between two people, the connection they make." She writes something down in her notebook. Is she recording the conversation or writing down comments about me?

"The longest-lasting relationships are those that share the most common interests and the same philosophy of life. Opposites may attract but they don't last. People of like minds make the best lasting relationships. It's a proven fact." I see her lips moving but the words coming out don't seem like their hers, at all.

"Did you major is psychology?"

"I read a lot. I'm a massage therapist."

Again, she makes more notes in her notebook and I'd kill to know what exactly she's writing about me. Even if she is only a massage therapist (which completely throws me, as I had taken her for an office professional of some kind), something bothers me about her whole theory of attraction. If what everyone really desires in a partner is someone that thinks like them, does the same things that they do and wants exactly the same things in life, then we are just secretly looking for a carbon copy of ourselves...in the body of the opposite sex. How creepy is that?

Could the entire notion of finding one's soul mate be a simple case of looking for ourselves in another body? Is the "soul mate" really just the best approximation of ourselves that we can find? Now that I think about it, I guess I've always felt most comfortable with a woman who shares the same or similar interests as myself and basically thinks along the same lines. I have had attractions to women that I considered very different to myself. It's true that although there was definite attraction and chemistry, we never made it past a few dates, either because we didn't communicate very well or, despite the good sex, we didn't particularly like each other.

Maybe Tracy is right (the studies do prove it, after all!). If so, I should narrow my search down to women that best resemble me. I wonder if that includes similarities in the looks department, as well, although that sounds a tad freaky? Wasn't it Narcissus that was cursed to fall in love with his own image and eventually died as a flower or something?

"I'll be right back," Tracy says and heads off to the bathroom. I nonchalantly pick up her notes and try to make out her handwriting. Out of nowhere, Tracy reappears and after giving me a disapproving look, grabs them back and takes them with her to the restroom. With that one act I know that the evening is blown. Whatever chance I had with her is irredeemably gone.

Like a young boy caught with his hand in the cookie jar, I look around the restaurant to see who may have witnessed my indiscretion and subsequent eye scolding. A very sexy brunette, whom I did notice before, seems to have witnessed everything; perhaps because she is alone she has more opportunity to people watch. Expressive eyes, voluptuous mouth, killer bod, I wonder why such a red hot sexy woman like her is dining alone. Did she get stood up?

Tracy returns from the restroom and immediately declares that she needs to leave, which she does. It's fine by me; I can always pick up a burger on the way home. As I slowly finish off my overpriced glass of cabernet, I could almost swear that the solo sexy lady just gave me a wry smile and then turned away. I wait for her to look back at me, for the longest time, but she doesn't: must have been my wishful thinking.

Before my next date I look up the term "Soul Mate" just to see what Wikipedia has to say on the subject. Apparently, the Greek philosopher, Plato had a lot to say on the subject. He believed that, at a time in the distant past, along with a head that had two faces, human beings also had four arms and four legs. The god, Zeus then split us humans into two parts, giving us our now distinctive one face, two arms and two legs. However, missing the rest of ourselves, feeling bereft in our completeness, we long for our other half or soul mate that we have been looking for in vain, ever since, in order to complete ourselves. Hmm. Maybe we are looking for our mirror image in another body, after all.

Susan is twenty-four in her profile and looks like she's thirty-something in real life. I take her to the same restaurant as the first strike-out, in the hopes that this time I will get to try their food. Here's the thing about meeting someone on a dating site: what looks and sounds good on paper does not necessarily accurately reflect what that person is like in reality. Susan, who looked classy and elegant in her photo is, in person, wearing so many beads, bangles, bracelets and rings that she looks like a walking jewelry store.

"My last boyfriend was very generous: a really big heart along with a really big wallet," she shares. "That's an irresistible combo to a woman, you know? Bought me this necklace on our second date. All these rings? He really knew how to treat a lady." Then she stares at me with an almighty, toothy smile. WTF?

I know where I stand with most guys but sometimes I have no idea where a woman is coming from. What is this woman saying? A guy that buys you jewelry is a keeper? In which case, where is her big-hearted big-spender now? Did he just declare bankruptcy, stripped of all cash, in debt and tapped out from buying her so much jewelry? Then maybe she figured that he didn't care for her anymore and so she dumped him? And why is she telling me this on our first date? Is it to let me know that the way to her heart is through Tiffany's?

"What happened with you guys? You and your ex?" I ask casually.

"I really don't want to talk about that," she answers, and her voice slightly quivers. Is that a tear in her eye? So, now

I'm thinking that, whether the breakup was in the distant past or more recent, she's not fully over him, which is fair enough. My guess is that he broke up with her and that she'd rather still be with moneybags, instead of sitting here with me and being back out on the dating scene, in general.

It's alarm bells all over the place for me and the way she got all teary at the mention of him suggests that to date her would risk involvement with an emotional basket case with a yen for crass jewelry. A soul mate, she is not.

Memo to self: change the online profile specifying the type of woman that I want to meet to sound exactly as if I'm describing myself.

She is cute though, and she has these amazing sad and vulnerable-looking eyes that are very expressive and incredibly sexy. I could easily imagine her in the bedroom; her dark hair a sexy mess and, a la Sophia Loren, those passionate eyes daring me to take her, body and soul.

As Susan continues to tell me about herself, I notice the entrance of the fancy rose seller. If you've never been on a date where a young woman wearing a flowing dress, Mediterranean style, strolls among the tables carrying a basket of single roses, with a cheap ribbon tied round it, don't fall for her charms: it's a scam.

Five and sometimes ten bucks for a single rose? Put a bearded guy on a stall outside selling single roses for that price and how many sales do you think he would make in a night? Maybe a couple of tourists, who just converted their yens and euros into the dollar, which is worth a fraction of their values and so to them is as close to worthless as monopoly money, would be takers.

What the cute young lady with the basket and the ribbons and the roses is counting on is that, on a date, the guy is vulnerable to emotional blackmail, especially if it is early in the dating process. What's a guy to do when the rose seller approaches your table, smiles at your date and says to you, "A rose for the lady?"

If you say, no thanks, you risk coming off looking cheap to your date, or worse, you make it seem like you don't think your date is worth the price of a flower. Even though *you* know it's an over-priced rose, you can't ask the rose seller, how much? If you do, then you better buy the thing because no matter how much the seller says, you can't say, no thanks, because then you're saying to your date that you were considering buying her a rose but not at that price because she ain't worth the five or ten dollars.

Asking how much is a lose-lose situation for a guy. If the rose seller says twenty dollars and you pay it, then your date is thinking that you're some kind of push-over and easily intimidated; you are a loser who will pay twenty dollars for a rose that could be bought in the store for a buck.

Luckily, I've perfected the win-win, ideal way of dealing with the whole, "Rose for the lady" situation: let the lady decide. If she's cool and in any way smart, she'll politely decline.

When the rose seller gets to us, sure enough, she smiles at Susan and asks me, "A rose for the beautiful lady?"

"Would you like a rose, Susan?" I ask with total innocence and lack of attitude. Susan doesn't say, no thanks, right away. She checks out the selection of roses; they're all different colors.

"They look very beautiful," Susan says, looking at me to see which way I'm going to go with it. I'm familiar with her inquiring look. It's the same look poker players give each other when looking to see what your tell is. I keep a non-committal half-smile on my face and give her a really hard read.

"How about this one?" the canny rose seller suggests, breaking up our Mexican standoff. Susan takes the rose from the seller and sniffs its scent. The rose seller instantly turns to me for payment.

"What do I owe you for the rose?" I ask, reaching for my wallet while looking at Susan to see if she's going to put the darn thing back.

"Fifteen dollars," answers the wily seller, which is bullshit because I overheard her tell another table nearby that the price was ten dollars.

"Didn't I just hear you say, ten dollars to that table over there?" I ask, politely.

"This is special rose," she says looking me straight in the eye, "fifteen dollars."

What choice do I have? I pay her off and make a note to myself to rethink the whole rose for the lady scenario.

"Thank you, Martin," Susan says appreciatively. "It's beautiful."

"It's special," I say. "Just like you." Susan puts down the rose and picks up the menu, totally missing my sarcasm.

I don't remember much more of the date except that she ordered two glasses of wine (from the wine list, not house), two appetizers and one of the more expensive entrees, all of which she couldn't finish and no surprise, asked for most of the food left on the table be nicely packed up to go home with her. I was thankful to end the date and kept my alcohol consumption to a minimum just in case I got guilt-tripped into stopping off somewhere on the way to her place to buy her some more jewelry.

Two dates and two strikeouts later, I am no closer to acquiring my hot-to-trot wedding date. I have one more rendezvous lined up. If that doesn't bear fruit, I'm back to where I started except with less funds in the bank.

It's Friday evening and I'm running late for my date. Earlier in the day, I had a job way out in West Covina, which is not my familiar turf and I ended up taking a picture of the wrong house. I had to drive back out there, find the right house and on my return got caught in heavy rush hour traffic. I didn't have time to shower or do much to get ready for my date but I did put some of Mike's product in my hair because I had a cowlick all day and no amount of brushing would get rid of it.

I'm not used to putting stuff in my hair and I managed to get rid of the cowlick but in exchange, after using some gel concoction in my hair, I look like I've just walked out of the sixties. It's a good look for Mike but on me it just looks goofy.

My date's name is Megan and she's a twenty-four year old executive. She looks really hot in her photo but couldn't be further from my interests so I'm not expecting much. Looking through her high powered resume again, now gives me the chills. Comparing my education and job history with hers, I look like a slacker. I'm running out of funds and I probably should cancel. She does look really hot, though.

I take Megan to the same restaurant because the prices are fairly reasonable, I know what to expect and there's nothing on the menu that's going to give me surprise sticker shock. Surprisingly, she looks just like her photo: really hot. Annoyingly, she keeps excusing herself to take incoming "important" phone calls.

"I want the complete financials on my desk first thing Monday morning, Warren. And that's financials for the past three years, not two. Until I get those, there's nothing to talk about."

While Megan is talking like she's Gordon Gekko's female protege from the movie, *Wall Street*, I notice the same sexy, older woman that I saw on a previous date, eating alone at the same table which she was sitting at before. Wait. Did she just smile at me, again?

"I'm so sorry," says Megan, hanging up, "you were saying?"

It's really strange to me how a beautiful woman can look so pretty, yet something about them: the way they talk, their scary opinions, or just their attitude, can rub me the wrong way. And the more they talk, the less beautiful they become. Visually, nothing has changed but it's as if the eyes or maybe the beauty appreciation center in my brain have adjusted Megan's looks score downward, from a ten to a six, or maybe even as low as a five. I can't help but frown to myself.

"I was wondering if you've seen the movie, *Wall Street*?"

"I don't have time to go to the movies," Megan answers.

"Wall Street is an old movie. It's considered a classic."

"Why do you ask? Why that movie?"

"It's about money and business. It has this famous speech where the lead character, Gordon Gekko played by Michael Douglas, convinces everybody that greed is good. You should get it on Netflix or online somewhere."

"I don't care for Michael Douglas. He's too old." Like I was asking her to date the guy and what does "too old" mean, anyway? Too old for what? He can't be too old to act, unless the character he's playing is supposed to be younger.

"Do you have herpes?" she asks.

"Do I have herpes? No, I don't have herpes, why would you ask me that?"

"I didn't say herpes, I said a hair piece. You look like you're wearing a hair piece, not that there's anything wrong with that."

"No, I put some stuff in my hair to try to make it behave but all I managed to do was make myself look like a poor man's James Dean." I smile at her and she frowns.

"Who's James Dean?" Seriously, this girl needs to get a life.

"He's an old actor, you wouldn't like him. He's so old, he's dead." I say with a straight face and more for my own amusement. Her cell phone buzzes again and she instantly checks the caller ID.

"I have to take this," she says, taking the call.

"Oh, hi," she answers, her tone instantly changing to one of sweetness and light, which is very disconcerting.

"I had a great time too," she continues, obviously now talking to a previous candid date, someone that she definitely likes. "Yes, I'd love to but I'm in a meeting right now, can I call you back?" She checks her watch and doesn't look at me, not even for a split second. "I'll be done here in like, thirty minutes."

She hangs up and without even an acknowledgement of her conversation or her presumptuousness in determining that she is dumping me in like, thirty minutes, closes her menu and casually asks, "Tell me about yourself," in a tone that is so uninterested, it is farcical.

Out of sheer menace and vindictiveness, I pull out my cell phone as if I am getting a call and hold up a finger, like I really have to take this. "Mike, so glad you called, I was just about to call you. No, so far I'm fine but I did leave the house without my medication again and I'm starting to hear the voices. Can you get them to me ASAP before I become a danger to myself and others?" I hang up and look at her, "sorry about that," I say. I see now that I've got her undivided attention.

"Is he coming?" she asks with concern.

"Nah," I answer while opening my menu. "He can't make it."

Megan quickly gets up to leave and immediately I feel like a shit and instantly regret the spontaneous lark, even if it was funny for a brief moment. "Hey, relax," I say with forced calm. "I was just goofing around."

"My brother is a schizophrenic," Megan practically yells at me. "You fucking moron."

I now feel so bad about the situation that I secretly wish she would turn around and, with an instant smile, say, "Gotcha." But she doesn't: she keeps walking right out the door.

As I watch Megan fade from view, I notice that the sexy lady has obviously witnessed the entire fiasco. She gives me a consolation prize smile, loaded with sympathy and humor, and this time, she doesn't look immediately away.

"I'm never going to get laid," I say to her, even if she is

out of earshot. Whether she understands or not, she returns another beautiful smile. I don't need a second invitation to go visit her. "I guess that's your table, huh?" I say to her as I attempt to channel Cary Grant.

"Creature of habit," she responds.

"You always eat alone?"

"Naw," she replies, as I notice what a beauty she is. "I used to do what you're doing."

"Touché," I say, thinking fast what my next pickup line should be. She is so beautiful, she could be a model: big brown eyes and gorgeous, silky, flowing brunette hair that you see on those TV shampoo commercials.

"What's your name?" I ask, playing it safe.

"Frances."

"Martin," I say, extending my hand. "Mind if I join you?"

"Please do," she says and I'm so surprised that, number one, I asked so casually and number two, that she said, yes. This whole thing is flowing so smoothly and so totally like a "meet cute" in the movies that... instantly, I'm smitten.

Conveniently, Frances has not yet eaten, either. So we both order from the menu and all of a sudden I'm on a date with a woman I had no idea even existed. I'm feeling very comfortable with Frances, almost as if I have known her a very long time. She doesn't seem to be sizing me up or making judgments about me in her head; if she is, she hides it very well.

In fact, she doesn't seem uptight about anything and seems very comfortable in my presence. Maybe because she is older, she has seen it all and is less stressed about anything. Maybe she doesn't consider this a date and she just wants the company?

"How's the dating going?" she asks me with such a cute mischievous grin that I feel a rush of emotion that makes me think that I've just fallen in love with her.

"Not too good," I answer. "But then, you're my key

witness, you saw me strike out at least twice."

"There were more?"

"Just one more. Online dating. I should ask for a refund."

"They were too young for you," she says as she places some food into her full-lipped, sensuous mouth. Is she flirting with me?

"Yes," I respond. "I should definitely be with someone older, someone more…mature."

"Why do you want to be with someone?" she asks and her serious question spooks me. I pause and then decide to come clean.

"I'm really trying to get a date to come to my ex-girlfriend's wedding. She sent me an invitation."

"And you're going to show?" she asks, incredulously.

"You don't think I should go?"

"Only if you show up with someone hot."

"Exactly, right?"

"Who have you got so far?" she asks but I pretend to chew my food longer than I need to in order to avoid an answer. "When is the wedding?" she then asks, sensing my embarrassment.

"Less than three weeks."

"What's the date?" she asks as if maybe she's considering it, is she?

"The twelfth. Why?"

"I'm not doing anything on the twelfth," she says and calmly takes a sip from her wine.

"You'd go? I mean, would you like to come? As my date?" and suddenly all my pretend maturity and sophistication abandons me, leaving behind what feels like an insecure six year old kid inside.

"Sure, why not?"

"Seriously?"

"Email me the details," she says and gives me the sweetest smile that totally melts my lonesome heart.

4. I ONLY WANT TO BE WITH YOU

After our amazing meal together, I don't want to leave the company of Frances so I invite her to a bar next door for a drink. She gladly accepts and one drink turns into many. The place is full and very lively; the only seats available are a couple of bar stools at the counter. I've sat on a bar stool at many a bar with my male friends but never with a date; it's always been at a table or a booth where we were both on our best behavior.

Frances is different. It's almost like she's one of the guys, yet she's the hottest chick I've ever dated. Even the word chick doesn't do her justice. She's a lady, yet it's as if she has no pretentions about anything. She slings her amazing, yet petite ass onto the bar stool like it was the most natural thing in the world and, without hesitation, orders us a couple of beers. I think I'm in love.

"What's up?" she asks me, as if she can read my mind.

"I was just thinking that I'm more used to women who will only sit at a table and sip a glass of house wine for the entire evening, all the while watching their Ps and Qs. And mine, come to think of it."

"I don't like Ps and Qs," she says, adorably. "What kind of woman have you been dating, anyway: uptight and boring?"

"Pretty much, I guess."

"I have a theory that a person's attitude towards women is formed the first time their heart gets broken."

She also seems to like a challenge. It's like she prefers the cut and thrust of conversation more than she does finding out answers in a typical question and answer kind of way. I need to keep up and not be boring.

"Tell me about the first woman that broke your heart

and I'll tell you how your attitude to love changed as a result."

Okay, Frances may have a few years on me, and obviously has had way more experience in the broken heart department than I, but I'm not going to make our age difference so obvious by telling her that I've had just one broken heart in my life or that it occurred only a few brief months ago. I don't want to think that maybe she is robbing the cradle, after all.

"I had a very unusual first love experience, as a matter of fact...very weird" I answer, stalling.

"Try me," she says, straightening in her seat, in expectation of a good yarn.

"It was in summer...on the beach," I say, wondering where I am going to go with this.

"What was on the beach?" she asks, her curiosity piqued.

"My first love."

"How old were you?"

"Fourteen," I quickly say and take a long swig of drink. "There was a sand sculpture competition. The entire beach was one long stretch of really neat sand sculptures. It was there that I met her."

"Who?"

"The woman of my dreams."

"Tell me about her."

"She had amazing breasts, I mean, an amazing face with very pouty lips and long flowing hair and curves, curves everywhere, just an amazing, sensual, naked woman, lying on the beach."

"You're describing a sand sculpture, aren't you?"

"I was in love, Frances. For the first time in my life I was in love. It may have been an impossible love, most tragic love stories are, but I couldn't help myself. Love knows no bounds."

"Agreed. Then what happened?"

"The attraction was so powerful, so magnetic, it was if I had to have her…"

"Eeeuw."

"I don't mean like that, I mean that I had to have her in my life, in my heart. I thought, then and there that if we were to be together, the gods would make it happen. I believed in magic, then."

"I'm feeling all teary already. What happened?"

"I kissed her."

"Nice. Did she have dry lips? Tell me you didn't French kiss…"

"Frances, you're ruining this," I say, mock chastising her. Frances raises her palms in mock apology. "She came alive," I continue. "She came alive with my kiss. Her eyes opened and what beautiful, soulful eyes they were. My heart…rejoiced."

"Rejoicing hearts are the best."

"I extended my hand to her, smiled a beautiful smile…she took it and I lifted her up…"

"Your love lifted her up. Beautiful."

"She stretched and yawned like she had been in slumber for eternity…"

"She was probably made fresh that morning but go on…"

Again, I mock chastised Frances and her lips smiled with a hint of naughtiness. I could tell that she was enjoying my little romantic, made up escapade and, hopefully, liking me better.

"She was the most beautiful vision I had ever seen. Hand in hand, we ran and…frolicked on the beach."

"I love to frolic," says Frances, unable to help herself.

"I was in bliss," I continue. "I took her down to the shore and we playfully cavorted…"

"If there's one thing I like better to do than frolic, it's to cavort," Frances says, lightheartedly. "What happened next?"

"I picked her up in my arms and took her to the water. Knowing I was going to dunk her, she squirmed in my arms, flailing her arms about, trying to break free."

"That's so playfully romantic."

"She screamed as I dropped her into the surf."

"You brute."

"My joy quickly turned to terror…"

"Oh, no. What happened? She turned into a sea lion?"

"Worse. She began to dissolve. She literally melted into the ocean, never to be seen again."

"You must have been devastated."

"I tried to save her by scooping up what was left of her but all I came up with were lifeless handfuls of wet sand."

"That's cruel. Did you yell at the gods for your misfortune?"

"I railed against the gods: why, why take someone so young and vibrant?"

"With curves everywhere and such an amazing rack. Tragic."

"My first broken heart," I say with exaggerated sadness. Frances smiles and appears to think deeply, as if putting on a therapist's demeanor.

"The sand girl is a metaphor for the type of woman you attract. You wake someone up with your love. They blossom in your attention but it never lasts. They vanish from your grasp like sand running through your fingers."

"Man, you're good," I say, matching her mock seriousness but inwardly meaning it.

"Stick to your own kind, Martin. Sand girls are trouble."

"Okay, your turn," I say. "Your first broken heart: I'll analyze you."

"His name was Scruffy," she says, right away.

"Scruffy?"

"He was a terrier. A terrier mix, I guess."

"I'm not talking about pets that broke our hearts when

they died."

"Me neither," Frances argues, "Scruffy was the first I had sex with." I almost choke on my beer. Have I judged her all wrong? Is she a pervert?

"You had sex with a dog?"

"He lived next door," she continues, calmly. "I never really noticed him till one day I was sent over to deliver some food to old Mrs. Birdwhistle."

"Where are you going with this?" I ask, a wee bit concerned.

"I entered her house with the plate of food and shouted out for her, 'Mrs. Birdwhistle?' She shouted at me from upstairs to wait, that she'd just be a moment. She could have been in the bathroom."

"How old were you?"

"Ten, eleven, maybe."

"This is so weird, go on."

"As I stood in her living room, a small, scruffy little dog came sniffing in."

"The aforementioned Scruffy, I take it."

"I was polite and probably would have petted him, had my hands have been free. He sniffed at my feet and without so much as a friendly greeting, he mounted one of my legs."

"Aw, jeez…" I squirm.

"I didn't know much about sex at that age but I knew enough to know that this strange dog was having his way with me."

"You must have been horrified."

"I was. But strangely, as the shock wore off, I realized that I had actually enjoyed it. The pleasure on his face as he was…it was exhilarating."

"I don't want to hear any more," I say and mean it. This is too weird.

"Love isn't always clean and clear cut, Martin. Sometimes the emotions can be very conflicted. I made several more visits to the house, delivering food for the old lady but I really just wanted to see Scruffy."

"What happened? Did you guys elope?"

"One day, I looked through Mrs. Birdwhistle's window and got the shock of my life."

"Mrs. Birdwhistle was dead on the floor?"

"Please," Frances mock admonished me, "don't be macabre."

"Sorry."

"I saw Scruffy cheating on me."

"With a dog?"

"No, my next door neighbor, Timmy Dolan. Scruffy had another lover. Maybe he was two-timing me all along, I don't know, but he broke my heart. I felt cheap and betrayed."

"That's pretty… shocking. Are you guys still in touch?"

"I did see him a few times after. He'd come up to me and act like nothing had happened. I never told him that I'd seen him that day."

"Wow. Well, I see how that could mess you up for life."

"What are your thoughts, doc?"

I pretend to light and smoke an imaginary pipe as I consider her bizarre tale.

"Let me see," I say with fake gravitas. "You feel that men are like dogs. If they get horny enough, they'll hump just about anything. You'll think that their love is special, that you are their only one. But then they'll cheat on you. Men will use you up and they can't be trusted."

"Pretty much sums up my experience. You're very good."

"Hence the solo dinners," I add, strengthening my evaluation.

"Touché, doc," she mock salutes. "Thankfully, they don't allow any dogs in the restaurant."

I laugh and hold up my beer glass in a toast: "To dogs and sand women."

"And broken hearts," Frances says as she clinks my

glass. As we exchange a long look and smile at each other, it really does feel like I've known this beautiful, sensual and fun, fun woman, since forever. Please god, don't let me fuck this up.

5. NEVER TAKE YOUR DATE TO A PARTY

I was busy with work the next few days but all I could think about was Frances. I was a bundle of excitement counterbalanced by a hefty dose of anxiety, all rolled up into one big mess of butterfly stew in my solar plexus. Part of me wanted to go full steam ahead and another part of me wanted to run away and flee. I decided to opt for a course mid-point between the two: proceed with caution.

There were a million things I liked about Frances; she is beautiful and sexy, tons of fun, and obviously very intelligent. Strangely enough, I didn't know which side of the ledger to put her intelligence on: is it a positive or a liability? I haven't been with that many women whom I could say were actually more intelligent than me and I'm not quite sure why I feel so intimidated. Is it simply that I am feeling like I have to mentally keep pace with her on our dates (which might get to be a bit exhausting) or is it that she will soon discover that I'm not as bright as she thinks I am and she'll then tire of me and find me boring?

In the meantime, I will have fallen seriously for her and then here comes heartbreak number two? And how old is she, anyway? She's gotta be in her thirties…is her age something that I can ask her about? Maybe I'm thinking about her too much and what if she's not thinking about me, at all? Am I just a little distraction for her until she finds a more serious candid date? Why is she single, anyway? I'm sitting on a park bench in my favorite park overlooking the ocean, the sunset is about to unfold and, instead of feeling mellow and relaxed inside, my head feels like it's just about to explode.

And why aren't I taking any photos of courting couples? What's happening to me? Is this what entering a new relationship does to a person, or is it just me? Am I going to let all my interests and my customary routines fall by the wayside and become obsessed instead with what Frances might be thinking and feeling about me? Should I call her? What if she's seeing other guys? She must get hit on, all the time. Why would she be interested in me? I should call her. If she's all weird and doesn't want to go out again, then that will be fine; it will be a relief, actually. I'm kinda hoping that she does blow me off. Who cares about bringing someone to the wedding? So, I look at the ocean to calm myself, take a few deep breaths and call her.

"Hello?" she answers.

"It's Martin."

"Hello Martin." As soon as she says my name and her tone is warm and welcoming, I calm down a lot. She actually sounds quite happy to hear from me. "I'm glad you called," she says. "I've been thinking a lot about you." Women put themselves out there emotionally way much more than guys. I love it.

"What have you been thinking?" I have to ask.

"Oooooh," she purrs, "yummy thoughts." Okay, all is great in my world.

"I've been thinking yummy thoughts about you, too," I say with absolute ease and calm confidence.

"What are you doing?"

"I'm on my way home from a job, just stopped by the park. I looked at the beautiful sunset and thought of you."

"You are a romantic chappie," she says, her voice intimate and affectionate. "I like it."

I smile to myself. This is fun. "What are you doing? As a matter of fact, what is it that you do...professionally?"

"I'm a production designer for stage and TV. I'm working on a stage design right now. It's driving me mad."

"How old are you?" I ask quickly.

"Thirty-eight."

"Really?"

49

"Is that ancient?"

"No, I'm sorry. I'm surprised because you look much younger. Not that thirty-eight is old, it's not, it really isn't…"

"It's all relative, isn't it?" Frances says, helping me out. "To you I may be old but I normally date older men and they think I'm young. My ex-husband is ten years older, as a matter of fact."

"You're divorced?"

"Yeah. Three years ago. I was married for fourteen."

"Wow. How come you guys broke up?"

"He left me for a younger model," she says with a hint of…bitterness? Even as I ask her questions, I realize that I am in over my head. This is an older, mature woman with a past. She has a history of relationship…I mean, god knows how many serious boyfriends she had before she got married. And she was married for how long? FOURTEEN YEARS?

"Are you there?" she asks.

"Yeah, I'm sorry, I…I have an idea. We keep interviewing each other like this and we'll just freak each other out and never get past a first date. Let's just spend some time together. Whatever gets revealed, gets revealed. Deal?" I am dead serious.

"Deal. I was freaking you out?"

"Just a little," I answer, dying to get off the phone.

"Before you go," she says, perhaps sensing my withdrawal, "want to come to a party Friday night?"

"Yeah, love to," I answer.

"I'll call you back with the details," she says and we hang up. As I put away my cell phone, I realize that I am impressed with how she handles me. I was freaked out by her answers and I would have ended the conversation and hung up without asking her out on a further date. Very smartly, she asked *me* out on a date and did it so casually, it was no effort for me to say yes. This is one smart cookie, I almost laugh out loud.

Friday couldn't come quick enough and then, when it came, it came too soon. In the apartment I had been keeping to myself, holed up in my room with Pandora streaming indie love songs which I'll never admit to anyone is my favorite genre station. I had two hours to get ready for the party and I hate to sound like a girl but I fully need two hours to do everything that I need to do to make myself look good.

I had already used up thirty of those precious minutes by staring into my wardrobe and pulling out clothes that I thought would be appropriate until I realized that I hadn't a clue about what was appropriate to wear. I had never been to a party for grown-ups before where, presumably, everyone was over forty and was going there to chat and meet people rather than get wasted and hook up with the nearest willing nympho. What do you wear to a grown-ups party? A dress shirt, a nice pair of slacks and a corduroy jacket with elbow patches? I don't have a single article of sensible clothing in my entire wardrobe.

I had heard Mike go the bathroom earlier on, so I was surprised to realize that he was still using it twenty minutes later. He had the door open because he wanted to hear if his phone rang. He was shaving when I gave him the nod that I needed to use the bathroom.

"You going out tonight?" he asks me when he sees me carrying my change of clothes, party clothes. "Haven't seen you around much."

"I love you, too," I say, inching my way further in.

"Are you dating someone?"

"Just met someone but I'm not sure yet if we're dating. Checking each other out, I guess."

"You haven't fucked yet, in other words."

"So nicely put."

"Do you want to fuck her?"

"I guess," I say, hoping for maybe some brotherly

advice. "I'm kinda scared."

"First time is scary," Mike says, sarcastically.

"Fuck you," I say jokingly but secretly mean it.

"I mean first time with a new chick. Not first time, ever. What are you nervous about?"

"I don't know. She's older than me."

"Older women are trouble. Remember Veronica? Always two steps ahead. Knew what I was going to say before I even thought about it."

"Veronica wasn't an older woman, what are you talking about?"

"She was two years ahead of us at college. That's a fact."

"Two years, yeah, that's ancient."

"You going to bring the new chick around? We can double date."

"Not tonight. We're going to a party."

"Her party or your party?"

"Her party. Why?"

"You know why a chick brings you to her party, right?"

"No, why?"

"To see if her friends will like you. It's a chick initiation. If her friends like you, you're in. If they don't…you're out. Unlike men, women need the approval of their friends."

"Great. Just what I need: more pressure. Thanks for the support, bro."

"You're welcome. Anytime."

Mike finishes what he's doing at the wash basin and leaves but quickly returns and places a condom on the sink. He gives me a thumbs up sign: "They're going to love ya!"

Frances said that she would come pick me up because the party was on my side of town and it was easier for her to swing by my place than to have me drive over to her, and then all the way back again, which makes perfect sense. Problem is, I'm not used to women I date making perfect sense. Most of them would insist that I pick them up no matter what the driving logistics were. Why is this chick so different? Does she act like a woman but think like a man?

Or maybe she's assuming I drive an old, beat up Japanese car (which, in all fairness, I do) and she'd prefer to be seen driving up in her luxury German sedan. Perhaps it's a control thing; if, for some reason, it doesn't go so well, she can simply drive herself home and not be dependent on someone else. I know so little about this woman, I should just try and chill and take it every minute at a time. She's late. What if she doesn't even show up?

Frances shows up driving a late model BMW and right away I decide that I don't belong in this relationship, if that's what it is. She greets me with a kiss and an amazingly warm hug and right away I feel like this is where I belong: in her arms. The rightness of our connection confuses me; why does our togetherness feel so good? I've never felt like this with any other woman, Roxanne included. Is Plato right? Is Frances my missing other half who makes me feel whole? It sure feels that way.

Frances looks amazing in a tight-fitting, cute, two-piece dress thing that I don't know the name for. She even drives like a man, with poise, focus and intent. I don't mean to sound sexist but all the women I've seen driving…well, they tend to be scatty, uncertain and especially terrifying when making a left turn or wanting to pull out into oncoming traffic. That includes my mom, so I know it's not an age thing.

Even the music she's playing is cool, young and hip. Most older people I know, well, let's just say that their musical tastes never made it past the eighties, blah. I made some positive comments about her musical tastes and we talk uncertainly about music that we like and don't like. I'm not sure if she is feeling it but we're really awkward with each other, which is a concern.

There's a few times in my life where I met some chick

at a bar with whom I had an amazing time with and we seemed to totally click. We'd go on a date a day or two later and it was like we were strangers from two different alien planets. We'd be so awkward with each other that after a few glaring pregnant pauses in conversation, we'd agree that it must have been the alcohol that tricked us into thinking that we were made for each other. In the cold, hard light of day, it was obvious that we more suited as contestants for the Mr. and Mrs. Mismatch TV game show than legitimate candidates for a lasting, long-term relationship.

I'm not saying that that's how I'm feeling towards Frances but there is a definite whiff of awkwardness among us. Maybe it's nothing a glass or two of wine won't fix. I'm pretty much assuming that this is not the kind of party that forces everybody to knock back half a dozen jello shots before the serious drinking begins but they've got to have some wine, right? I have no idea what to expect and I'm really thinking that going to a party on our second date is not a good idea. We should have gone the traditional route with dinner and a movie instead, which is much less pressure and it would give us a chance to first explore and then cement our togetherness.

Apart from the fact that the party attendees are going to be all her friends, going to a party with your date is a very risky proposition. Every party that I've ever gone to with a date has had one main hazardous drawback: there are far too many single men on the prowl.

Let's face it, hosting a party is really agreeing to turn your pad into a meat market for the evening. Some may argue that no two parties are the same but as far as my limited experience goes, as far as I can tell, all parties are exactly the same: a party is a formalized mating ritual which facilitates the hooking up of single people in a socially acceptable way.

Picture the scene… people begin arriving and quickly decide to form themselves into various, individual groups:

coupled people, single guys and single gals. The coupled people only group with other couples that they know and pretty much exclude themselves from the real meaning of the party.

Single guys will form their group, not in the kitchen or any other secluded part of the house, no, they will gather wherever the single women are. Pretending to be interested in each other, what they really are doing is checking out every woman in attendance, single or accompanied. Single women form their own group and do exactly the same.

As every man knows, unaccompanied, single women at parties are usually not very pretty. If they are, then, generally, there's something wrong with them, maybe some emotional damage you'd rather not involve yourself in.

Attractive women always come with a guy. It doesn't matter whether she's into the guy or not, cute chicks will always be accompanied. It's the accompanied women that men most like to hunt at parties.

A single guy will already have pinpointed one or more women worth hunting. He will tell jokes and goof around with the single guys, all the while keeping his eye on the attractive women. What he's waiting for is that cute, accompanied woman to leave her group or date. When she does, she becomes immediately vulnerable and subject to approach.

Meeting her at the drinks table, casually, as if by accident, he musters up all the charm he can with the express purpose of making her laugh. As every guy knows, if you can make the cute chick laugh, she is entirely stealable. If her date doesn't see the danger signs and catch on pretty quickly, then he's going home alone or maybe with that other boring couple he's being so chatty with.

As I think about this, a horror scenario erupts in my head. I'm at this party with Frances and I know by looking at the guys that already she has made at least three single guy's hit list. We're sitting/standing at an armchair talking to a couple that she knows and I'm drinking too much but managing to be polite in conversation and successfully giving the impression that I'm a perfect match for Frances. Meanwhile, out of the corner of my eye, I'm keeping watch on the guys that I know have Frances locked into their sights.

Aside from perfect vigilance, taking a woman to a party requires excellent bladder control. Unfortunately, in the scenario in my mind, I have drunk too much and finally I can no longer hold it in. I must find somewhere to pee. I excuse myself, find out where the bathroom is and hurry upstairs through a pokey hallway where the newly acquainted single people can flirt and get to know each better away from the maelstrom of the other hunter-gatherers downstairs.

There's a line for the bathroom and every woman that goes in takes an age to come back out again. My heart starts beating faster with every minute spent away from Frances. I can imagine every single guy in the place, positioning themselves closer to her group: people they would never normally be interested in, even if they were the last people on earth.

When I finally get my chance to relieve myself, I rush downstairs and instantly check out the armchair where I just left her: it's empty. My heartbeat increases as I rapidly scan the room, seeking her presence. She is nowhere to be seen. I try not to panic as I come up with possible places where she might be. She could have found that secret bathroom that every party seems to have, the hidden downstairs half-bathroom, the one only the females seem to know about.

Or maybe she's in the kitchen, exchanging cheese dip recipes with the host's mother and the elderly next door neighbors. But deep down, in my gut, I know…she's been stolen.

When I finally find her, my heart flat lines: it's worse than I'd imagined. Sitting on the stairs at a party is like putting up a 'do not disturb' sign on the motel room front door, yet there she sits in bubbly conversation with a cosmopolitan, wealthy guy who looks like he just walked off the front page of GQ Magazine. Worse still, their knees are touching, which is a very bad sign.

I know that the thing to pay attention to in these types of situations is how she reacts when she sees me. If she runs down the stairs, swings her arms wildly around me and plants a big kiss on my lips, I will know that my fears are irrational and that I have been totally overreacting.

When Frances finally breaks her gaze away the most handsome man in the world, she reacts like her fun is over and that it's now time to go back to doing the laundry.

"Hi, Martin," she'll say, "I want you to meet Roger..." but she doesn't know his last name which tells me that they have just met.

"Papasmear," the guy will help out, "Roger Papasmear."

Of course he'll say it with some continentally inflected accent that makes the last name sound sophisticated and not, well funny. As he talks about the economy or some such gibberish, I'm not able to tell if he's from Paris, Sicily, Timbuktu or is merely a recent immigrant to the oppressed people's ghetto on the other side of town where he's sleeping rough with some fellow ex-pat winos.

"We should get going," I'll say to Frances as she reluctantly extracts herself from his deadly charms. I will feel like a parent who has just ruined his daughter's life by embarrassing and telling her, in front of the hot, mature guy, that it's way past her bedtime.

"Where did I leave my coat?" Frances will say as a ruse to get me to go find it and leave them alone for a few more seconds. I don't fall for it, as I know how critical it is not to leave them alone for any further intimacy. Standing watchful of them both should prevent the dreaded exchange of business cards (the grow-up version of scrawling your phone number on a prospective date's palm with a ball point pen).

"Let me give you my card," Papasmear says brazenly, almost sneering at me, as if he fears little for my proximity and, at this stage, fails to take me seriously as a rival. If Frances offers up one of her cards in exchange, I will know that I am history. She goes one step further and writes her personal number on the back of one of his cards. I am so toast.

"What are you thinking?" asks Frances, taking me out of my finely constructed mental horror story, "you're miles away."

"Oh, nothing. Just wondering what this party is going to be like."

"To be honest, I'm kinda apprehensive about bringing you."

"How come?" I ask.

"All day long I've had these images of how disastrous it could turn out to be."

"What kind of disastrous images?"

"We're at the party and it's going fine, we're talking to some people. But at some point I go to the bathroom. It takes a while because it's mostly women that are using it. When I come back, you're not where I left you. You go missing. So I go looking for you and I eventually find you outside by the pool, sharing a hammock with some ditsy twenty-year-old cheerleader type.

"So I'm thinking maybe I'll just leave you there and go home. I then decide that I'll be braver than that and so I go up to you and immediately regret it. Your reaction to seeing me is to act like your father just opened the bathroom door and caught you jerking off to a girlie magazine. The cheerleader seems to think that I'm your aunt or something, and she brazenly writes her phone number in a crudely drawn heart on your wrist with a Sharpie."

Frances smiles at her own horror scenario, which relaxes me into a state of abject mellowness. She even thinks like me. She's gotta be "the one."

"I guess I'm afraid someone young and really cute is going to make a play for you," says Frances and smiles over at me.

"Forget it, Frances," I console her. "Not going to happen." I smile reassuringly to her. Something has shifted with us and we both have grown more comfortable and calmer with each other. She smiles back and I reach out and place my hand on top of hers, which I can tell, she likes. We're so clicking.

When we finally get to the party I'm not surprised at how civilized the whole thing is. What I am disappointed, and taken aback by, is that people over forty don't seem to know how to party. First of all, there's no keg of beer. Having a party without providing a keg of beer is like inviting someone over for thanksgiving dinner and not serving turkey: it's a wash. Why? Because not only does a keg of beer provide unlimited booze for everyone for the entire evening but it's also the grand central meeting point around which everyone circulates and gets to know everyone else at the party. No keg. No beer. No fun.

Another disappointment is that these older folks don't drink; okay, so maybe they have one or two drinks which they sip on for the whole evening and no one, not one single person gets drunk and goes on a screaming rampage through the house or running up and down the stairs carrying his best buddy over his shoulder. Boring.

I don't see anyone sneaking around to the rear of the house to throw up or pee in the bushes when the line for the bathroom gets too long. And where's all the single guys? There are maybe one or two single guys but I suspect that their sexual orientations are questionable; not one of them seems interested in hitting on women, single or accompanied. Granted, I don't see any single women, hot or unattractive, either. It seems that everybody here is coupled already, probably all married since forever.

Aside from a few waves to people she knows and a

couple of quick hellos, Frances stays real close to me and holds my hand the entire time, which makes me feel really wanted. She also seems to be engrossed in everything I have to say, as if my opinions about everything and anything really matter. Her attention and the way she engages me makes me feel like I'm important and have things to say.

We talk exclusively to each other and I can't remember the last time that I've had such a connection with someone. We talk about subjects that I never seem to get to talk about to my friends: the state of the American economy, where we're going, and how civilizations seem to rise and fall in a cyclical way; places in the world that we can't wait to visit; celebrity culture and the dumbing down of the American civilization; the best freeways and shortcuts to take in L.A. getting from her side of town to mine …the discussion is riveting.

And movies. No conversation in L.A. is complete without discussing the latest movies and the general decline of movie-making in America. From movies in general, we drift into favorite movie genres. Hers is romantic comedy and to her, and only to her, do I admit that this is my favorite movie genre also. Don't get me wrong, I like a good action movie (as long as it's not about a super hero with comic book magic powers, whose appeal I just don't get) but I *love* the warm and squishy feeling in my heart when I watch a good romantic comedy.

We then talk about romantic love, something that I've been ruminating over this recent while.

"Romantic love is what we're conditioned to believe *is* real love," Frances says. "Life's a bitch until you find your one true love? Then, when you find that one person, you magically live happily ever after? It's a crock."

"It's a fairy tale," I agree. I don't mention it but I secretly believed that Plato was wrong.

"It's a myth and it's totally responsible for the annihilation of adult relationships in the twentieth century."

"Say, what?" I say, not following her at all. I stare, riveted at this beautiful and unbelievably intelligent woman.

"We've so bought into the romantic relationship fairy tale," France continues, on fire as she delivers her thoughts as quickly as they come to her. "We're told that we're miserable without it and that it's the only thing…*the* only thing that can bring us true and lasting happiness." Oh, now I get it.

"I'm up shit's creek until I meet my "Princess" and you're screwed until your "Prince" comes along."

"Exactly," Frances concurs. "Think of the pressure that puts on modern day relationships."

Suddenly realizing that we are one of the few couples left at the party, with just a nod of acknowledgement toward each other, we both finish our drinks and leave the party, still heavily engaged in our riveting conversation. There is no break in thought or discussion, even when we got into the car.

"Romantic love has its place, don't get me wrong," continues Frances, "but to define relationship solely in romantic terms is like describing marriage only by what a couple does on their honeymoon."

"Wow, that's so true. I've never heard it being put like that… in those terms before."

We get to Frances' apartment, in what seems like no time, and she automatically opens the door and we both casually walk in, still engrossed in our conversation.

"We can blame it all on the movies," I pontificate, "but in fairness, who wants to see a movie about a middle-aged married couple with a bunch of average, well-behaved kids? People pay to see romance. The audience wants that warm and gushy feeling in their hearts that only a romantic movie can deliver."

"That may be so," says Frances, I can see her thinking, digging deep to find her most succinct thoughts, "but how many times can they tell the same story? Boy meets girl.

Boy loses girl, then…just as girl is about to board an airplane out of town and out of his life, boy runs through the airport in a mad dash and panic, tracks her down, delivers some teary-eyed reason why he needs her so much which invariably melts her heart so much so that she tears up her ticket, changes her life and her plans in order to commit to a relationship that wasn't working in the first place…"

Frances stops talking at this point and looking sad, adds: "Don't get me started…" I have no idea what she means but I hesitate to ask.

"What are the most exciting parts of a relationship?" I ask as Frances pours two glasses of red wine. "The beginning and the end," I answer myself. "In the beginning, they want to have sex. In the end, they want to kill each other. In the middle? They go grocery shopping. In the movies, of course, they edit out the middle and leave in the sex and violence." Proud of myself, I take a sip of wine. Then I notice that Frances either isn't that impressed with my thought process, is tiring or just plain losing interest in the conversation.

"Exactly," she says, weakly.

"I guess we solved the whole romantic love enigma," I say smiling but uncertain.

"I guess we did," Frances says, as if her mind is ruminating upon other thoughts, elsewhere. "What are you in the mood for?" she then asks, her voice low and sexy.

"You mean like coffee versus wine or something?" I respond, nervously. Frances deliberately puts down her drink and moving closer, looks directly into my eyes: she wants me to kiss her. I also put down my drink and slowly move my head closer to hers. I move slowly, just in case I've got the signals all mixed up and she really wants a shoulder massage or something, or worse, is giving me a hint to leave, instead.

As our lips meet, I realize that my lower lip is almost trembling. Unable to control it, I'm hoping that she doesn't notice. She doesn't seem to mind as her kissing becomes more passionate, which really gets me turned on.

I can hear the orchestral music soundtrack in my head as my body merges with hers, my chest caressing her full, soft upper body and I'm loving every moment of it. It has been so long since my body has had sex; I can feel my body's hunger and expectation. I can also feel Frances' hunger for me, which is such an intense turn on that I'm beginning to fear premature ejaculation.

Realizing where we're going with this, I consider that the hardwood floors are not at all appropriate for what's about to happen. We need the softness and aromatic sweetness that only a woman's bedroom can provide. I straighten my spine and, with the full-blooded, masculine image of Rhett Butler in my head, I scoop up my Scarlett in my big strong arms and without so much as a by-your-leave, m'am, I transport a willing Frances up the few small stairs and into the first door that is ajar which I am betting is her bedroom. Luckily for me, it is.

Placing her firmly, if not a tad roughly on her bed, with a full sexy, melodramatic flourish, I whip off my shirt. I am going to give Frances such a night of sheer, unabashed pleasure, the memory of which will stay with her forever. Without taking my lustful eyes off of an enraptured Frances, I unloosen my shoelaces and kick my shoes free of my feet. Unbuckling my belt buckle, with purpose and intent, in my head I am now an irresistible and irrepressible Elvis Presley in his younger years.

"What are you doing?" asks Frances, her tone of voice stops me cold in my tracks. The accompanying orchestral soundtrack's needle (which was just reaching a crescendo in my head), scrapes off of the vinyl LP.

"What?" I ask, in a voice that is now closer to Woody Allen's.

"We just spent the past few hours talking about the myth and triviality of movie romance and here you are, acting it out…movie sex." Frances sounds more disappointed than angry but either way, the total 180 degree change of direction throws me for an absolute loop.

"This is movie sex?" I ask, now feeling like an awkward seventeen-year-old.

"The orchestra plays, he carries her to bed, rips off his clothes, the curtains waft due to some imaginary wind and in a soft, luminescent light, they both come at the same time."

"Sounds good to me," I say, wondering what her problem is.

"Martin, that's not making love to me." Frances says softly and by her soft tone, I know that she's trying not to hurt my feelings. "That's more like you're playing out some fantasy in your head."

Feeling rejected, if not a little humiliated, I slowly put my clothes back on. "I'm confused," I say, unsuccessfully trying not to sound totally deflated. "If you didn't want to have sex, why did you come on to me, like that?"

"I do want to make love to you, Martin. But I want it to be real."

"I wasn't being 'real'?"

"No, Martin. You were giving a performance."

"Wow," I say with all of the petulance that I didn't know that I had. "Nothing like a harsh critic to brutally bash opening night performance." I know I'm being childish and maybe unreasonable, especially when I know in my heart that she isn't trying to bash me, but I'm hurt and can't seem to stop myself from lashing back with immature petulance. In fact, I feel like getting the heck away from here as fast as my feet can take me and I don't care how I'm going to get home.

"Where are you going?" she asks with concern and for the first time I hear uncertainty in her voice.

"The mood's broken," I say, still trying to find my other shoe. "I'm going to leave while I still have a semblance of male ego left." Which is only partly true. Perhaps the main reason I want to leave is because the momentous sexual desire which I had for her earlier on managed to find a shovel somewhere in the fertile crescent of my libido and proceeded to dig a hole so deep that it jumped right in and covered itself over with a mountainous size of densely compacted earth. Translation: if I stay and we get sexual again, I won't be able to get it back up. Rather than face that further humiliation, I feel that it is more prudent to flee.

I take a taxi and all the way home, sitting in the back, I feel woefully sorry for myself. What is her problem? You don't criticize a guy's performance the first time out. I had to leave. So what if she thinks I'm immature; no way could a guy get it up after a critique like that. And I was *really* looking forward to having sex.

6. HOW TO DRIVE A WOMAN CRAZY IN BED

Luckily for me the next few days were busy with work. I have a job for an advertising company pushing some line of third rate breakfast cereals which nobody has ever heard of. Maybe they are for the foreign market, Bulgaria or Turkey or some such country, I don't much care. I'm just here to take their photos.

I've been trying not to think of Frances, but it's next to impossible; all I can see in my mind's eye is her gorgeous, soft and vulnerable brown eyes looking forlornly at me as I run from her bedroom. What is wrong with me? Maybe I'm just not relationship material and I should just stick to short-term romances, not that I'm getting a lot of opportunities at those, either.

I really don't have a lot of sexual experience. I suppose that I was a little…no, a lot intimidated by the vastly superior sexual history of an older woman. Does every guy fear being laughed at by their sexual performance? Why do they refer to it as a performance, anyway? Performers need an audience and having an audience "watch" a performance turns every person in attendance into a critic. I'd hate to read the reviews of some of my past performances, that's for sure. I can only imagine what the headline for last night's performance would be: "Lead performer forgets his lines and runs offstage with his arms flailing about in the air, shouting, "run away, run away.""

Should I call Frances and apologize or something? What would I say? I'm sorry but last night I was a little off my game, better performances to follow? But then, I think to myself that last night was just one of those times that a guy can't recover from. As soon as I left, I imagine that she thumped her pillow hard several times and shouted, "stupid, stupid, stupid, what am I doing trying to have a relationship with an adolescent?" I think that I've blown it with Frances. I should move on.

I'm working with a very small crew and the really cute assistant, Cindy, is holding up an opened box of cereal before my camera, waiting for the director to cue her before she pours the cereal into the bowl. She keeps getting it wrong but it's not her fault. The director wants the cereal to flow down in a certain way. However, the way that the cereal flows from the aperture of the box, subject to gravity and current barometric pressure is really beyond the poor girl's control.

On the sixth attempt, I feel like telling the director that the whole idea is lame and he's better off using video and picking a frame from that footage so he can manipulate it in photoshop to get his so desired, "perfect" image, but I don't. It's my experience that director's hate my – or anyone else's – input. Maybe because they feel that taking advice from others makes them look like they don't know what they're doing, which, in many cases, they clearly do not.

"And pour," cues the director. Cindy tilts the box but nothing happens. She panics and madly shakes the box. The entire contents of rice crispies come spilling out and cause a total mess. I keep taking shots because I think the images look really neat and might work for some random photo collages that I sometimes put together, just for fun.

"Oh, shit, I am so sorry," Cindy apologizes, yet again. As the crew clean up and the director retreats to the craft services table, I take the opportunity to console her.

"It's okay, don't worry about it," I tell her, instantly making her feel better. "It's a much more difficult shot than it looks and we'll probably need, like, fifty takes to get the exact shot that he's looking for. This is perfectly normal, trust me," I say, wielding my "been-there, done-that," man of experience, tone which sometimes works for me, especially with interns and newbies. The way she relaxes and looks at me makes me think that I may be in with her.

"I'm not usually like this. Today, I'm like, total butter fingers," Cindy says sweetly.

"You must be in love," I say, flirting and fishing, all at the same time.

"I wish," she says. "I'm married."

As the director comes back for take seven, I mentally try to make sense of her reply. Was she saying that because she's married, she isn't in love? Or was she saying that she couldn't flirt back because she is married? Either way, she is a dead end, I reckon: she's married.

As much as I try to forget about my recent escapade with Frances, the whole sexual performance issue just keeps gnawing away at my brain. How does one know if one's performance is a good one?

Presumably, the woman that you're performing with is your number one critic and hence should give useful feedback as the event proceeds. What kind of feedback have I been getting? I rack my memory, trying to recollect reactions that I got from girlfriends while doing the deed. I'm not at all sure. In fact, I'm kind of appalled that I have barely focused upon and can hardly remember their reactions to my amorous efforts. I guess I just assumed that if I was having a good time, they were having a good time, too. I mean, nobody complained, so I must have been doing okay. Right?

Maybe I need to brush up on my technique, although I'm not sure exactly what my technique is or even if I have one. It's not like they teach it in school; how's a guy to learn if not through trial and error? Should I be reading books about it? Is it really lame if I have to buy some book whose title is, How To Make Love To A Woman? A primer.

How could I possibly look a cute clerk in the eyes if I brought that title up to the register at the book store? Maybe give her a wink and ask for her digits? I'd be a laughing stock. Maybe I'll swing by the library and take something out at the self-checkout where no one will notice.

The non-fiction, how-to book that I settle on is called, *How To Drive A Woman Crazy In Bed* by Marti McNeice. I'm assuming that Marti is a woman and that the book is written from a woman's perspective. If it's written by a guy, I would feel very suspect as how could I be certain that what he's writing, the purported wisdom that he's imparting in the book, has the agreement and approval of women? Otherwise, it could be just the male bragging of some guy who thinks he's god's gift to women. I'm not a dummy.

I decide to go to bed early and take the book with me. I'm half thinking that, considering the subject matter, I might get turned on and would need to be in a private space for that kind of pleasurable reading experience. I'm not sure what the definition of erotica is but surely reading a book all about sex must come pretty close, especially if there are pictures, which indeed, there are.

I'm half-way through the introduction when the real action starts next door: Mike and Gloria are at it again.

I had intended to ask Mike to move his bed further away from our adjoining wall because of the incessant thumping when the bed goes a rockin' but I couldn't find an appropriate segue way that would take me into a by-the-way, the noise you guys make when you're having fabulous sex disturbs me (and I'm not having any and I'm trying to sleep or sometimes read a book about how to have fabulous sex with an imaginary woman), so if you wouldn't mind...

So, I smirk to myself at the irony of it all: me reading about driving a woman crazy in bed while Mike is driving Gloria crazy in his bed, ha, ha.

The self-imposed, congenial bonhomie doesn't last, however. As soon as Gloria's loud moaning begins, my appreciation for the irony of the situation soon evaporates. Rather than screaming maniacally into my pillow, which is my first impulse, I decide instead to head out to the front room to watch Letterman on TV and crack open a cold brewski. "Oh, god, yes! Yes! Yes!" I hear Gloria's ecstatic declarations as I exit my bedroom.

Next day, I've no work so I take my camera and the book to the park and then to a nearby coffee shop. It's not my regular coffee shop so I don't expect someone I know to see me reading a how-to guide about how to do it properly. Out of the corner of my eye, I see group of twenty-something women at a table inside who seem to be nudging each other, looking my way and laughing. Although I'm not ruling out abject paranoia about reading such an embarrassing tome in public, I do cover the title with my hands. Better to be safe than mocked.

"Hey Martin, bro!" I hear and look up to see my old buddy, Jason, pulling up a chair at an adjacent table. He's accompanied by two of his, also hip, buddies. Jason was someone I wanted to be when I grew up and he managed to go where I could only dream: he became a photographer of super models.

We were in photography school together, with him being in the ultra cool clique and me an unofficial member of the geek clique. Under normal circumstances we would never had hung out together. I was dating Roxanne at the time and she was good friends with Jason's girlfriend, Debbie, so we got to play fake friends for a bit, while secretly despising each other.

"Hi, Jason," I say. "What's going on?"

As he settles with his buds, he asks me if I'm on my own, which I take to mean that if so, I should come join them. This, I do not want to do. So I tell him that I'm waiting for someone and that she's late.

"What's the book?" he asks, trying to make out the title.

"It sucks," I say, closing and hiding the cover.

"What's it called?"

"It's garbage," I answer and I actually throw it into the

garbage and pull my chair over to their table in order to deflect further scrutiny.

"Meet my buddies," Jason says, "Conrad and Jordan." As I shake the hands of the pair of uber-chic, cool, financially loaded hipsters, I briefly wonder if parents are aware of the possible life paths that their kids take based simply upon what names they give them. When they decide to forego the more common, generic names, like Mike or Steve, and branch out a bit into the cool baby names, like Zayden or Beckett or Ryland (Conrad, Jordan and Jason also qualify), are they aware of the future, greater life success that their kids will be given, simply based upon their cool names?

"We're all working on this huge shoot together, an international super fucking model fest, making shitloads of money," continues Jason. "What are you up to, man?"

"I, um...I'm doing good," I say. "Things are good."

"Martin went straight," Jason says to his buds, "decided not to do fashion."

Both Conrad and Jordan look at me like I'm nuts.

"That's where the money is, bro," says Conrad like he's talking to an idiot.

"What kind of stuff do you shoot?" asks Jordan, wondering if he's missing something.

"Industrials," I say, very matter-of-factly, "print...weddings."

Conrad and Jordan both look like they're trying to wipe the entire conversation from their minds, as they immediately lose interest and look around for something a tad more stimulating.

"Hey, Jay," says Conrad, grinning. "Check out these chicks."

Jason turns to check out the said chicks, who are the same ones inside the coffee shop, now giggling amongst themselves and presumably exchanging shameful comments about the three dishy guys talking to the poor schmuck who is studying about how guys like these drive hot women like them crazy in bed.

"Which one do you want?" continues Conrad. I'm not sure at what level of seriousness he asks the question, although I don't doubt for a moment that Jay or any of these boys could score with any of these women if they wanted.

"The one with the rack, man," responds Jason, who I now take to be the breast man among the group.

I watch as the three men slowly regress to horny teenagers and, through the window, visually engage the gaggle of chicks on the other side of the glass. The women are equally engaged and encourage the male attention with their laughs and giggles.

I wonder if the only reason that men and women express interest in each other is because of sex? Let's say that nobody, male or female, had a sex urge. Would the two sexes even bother getting together? Beyond sex and mating, what would they see in each other? Would they be even interested in each other?

"Which one would you sleep with, Martin?" enquires Jason.

"In accord with the natural pecking order of things, I would sleep with whatever women you guys don't want to sleep with." My response elicits a genuine laugh from the guys and, for a moment, I feel an elevation in group status. "Let me ask you something," I say, now that I have their attention. "Do you have any female friends that you just hang out with? Chicks you like but that you don't have sex with?"

"Why would I?" asks Jason, looking like he doesn't understand the question or maybe he does but thinks that it's a really dumb question to ask.

"I'm just curious," I say. "What about you guys? Are either of you just friends with women you're not screwing?"

"I've got two sisters, already," responds Jordan. "Why would I want another one?"

"I hang out with a chick that I'm not fucking," proffers

Conrad.

"Yeah?" I ask in a tone that suggests, please go on.

Conrad makes a fist with his left hand. "This is her," he says. He sticks out the index finger of his right hand, "This is me." He then shoves his index finger into the fist, to suggest screwing. "This is me in two weeks," he says, smiling broadly.

Clearly amused, his buddies slap him high-fives. I mentally calculate how long it will take the guys to have their coffees, flirt some more with the women, have the women join them, have some more coffees and then pair up and head off somewhere to party. ..

I realize that there is no way that I can sit here or even adjourn to another table and outlast them in order to retrieve the library book from the trash. I will have to consider it a lost cause and think of a really good excuse to give the librarian as to why I lost a book with such a titillating title. Nothing comes to mind right away.

7. ZEN AND THE ART OF RELATIONSHIP

Back at the apartment, I do some work on my 'look of love' project. As I look at photo after photo of joyful couples, I'm beginning to wonder if I'll ever have what they have. Why does it seem so free and easy with these couples? What did they have to go through to get to this point in their relationship? Were there challenges or did it all flow naturally? Do they have a different makeup than regular folks? Less resistance to giving and receiving love, maybe?

Am I actually lovable? I read somewhere that you have to love yourself first before someone else will love you. Is that true? I can safely say that I like myself but I'm not so sure about the loving part. I'd certainly prefer to be me rather than most people I know, actually probably more than anybody. I might envy good looking, successful people, like Jason, but would I want to *be* Jason? No, I wouldn't. Despite his charm and his confidence (bordering on arrogance), his sex appeal and hugely high success rate with amazingly beautiful women, I think that he's shallow.

Unless they're filthy rich, are guys like me relegated to date middle of the road women…and never get a look-in with the super hot, knockout babes?

Do I even want a super hot girlfriend? Well, of course I do, but at what cost? Never allowed to be my total self, I'd probably have to pretend to be resolute in my maleness and super confident all of the time, never letting them see any insecurities or chinks in my mental armor. What kind of meaningful relationship would that be? I could never be me.

But then, maybe I'm selling all the super hot babes short and underestimating their genuineness and authenticity by believing that they are only interested in superficial success. Then again, have I ever seen a super hot babe with a geeky guy that wasn't filthy rich? Not lately.

My cell phone rings: it's Frances. For some strange reason my heart jumps into my throat. What's that about? Should I answer it? What does she want to say? Does she want to vent and tell me off: what a lousy lover I was and then I ditched her and didn't even have the decency to call her the next day or the day after that to apologize and say that it's not her, it's me, I'm the guilty one, I'm a criminal for failing to perform to her satisfaction.

"Hello," I finally get the guts to answer and take my medicine.

"Hello, Martin," she says, all soft and warm and without a trace of anger, resentment or regret. Again, her voice melts me.

"I'm sorry for leaving like that," I say meaningfully.

"I'm sorry for being so insensitive," she says and by the way she speaks, so softly and sexily, I get the impression that she's lying down on her bed maybe watching *Sleepless in Seattle* for the hundredth time. "I had a lovely evening," she continues.

"What are you doing?" I ask after what seemed like a long, but not awkward pause.

"I'm lying on my bed, reading."

"What are you reading?"

"It's called *Zen And The Art Of Relationship*."

"What's it about?" I ask, realizing that's it's a stupid question which I left a bit too late to stop.

"It's a non-fiction book about applying Zen principles to romantic relationships." I have no idea what that might be, or mean, so I am stuck for an immediate follow-up question to ask. "Do you know about Zen?" she asks.

"A little bit...I've heard of it...no, not so much."

"It's all about being aware, being in the moment and being mindful of our thoughts and our feelings in the moment, the present moment. I love Zen. It's simple but very profound at the same time. But it's ultimately very simple."

"That clears it up entirely," I joke.

"I know, I know," she laughs. "I didn't explain it very well. I find that it's actually hard to define, you really have to do it and experience it for yourself."

"I'd love to," I say, with implied double meaning that I'm hoping she gets.

"What are you doing this weekend?" she asks, getting it. "Maybe you have some time?"

"I have all the time in the world…for you, Frances." I'm sure I can hear her smile.

"That's perfect. I'm driving up north for a family thing. It's my mother's seventieth birthday. Want to come?"

"For the weekend?"

"I'd love you to come. We can stay at my sister's place. It'll be fun. Might take you out of your funk. Oh, I've got a call coming through. Think about it and call me back."

I don't need to think about it: I'm in. Wait, she thinks I'm in a funk?

Again, Frances drives her very swish and comfortable Beemer while I sit in the passenger seat and enjoy the scenery as we drive north. She looks amazing. What's even more amazing is that, in her casual jeans and t-shirt, she looks like she's not even trying to look good, she just does. She has music playing that I don't recognize except to describe it as happy music and not at all what I would listen to normally.

I find myself conscious of being too cheerful about everything she says and generally smiling too much. I'm not sure if I'm doing it because a) I'm happy, b) I'm trying to be happy or c) I'm trying to appear like I'm not in some sort of funk or depression.

I would never categorize myself as being a depressed person but I don't know how I'm coming across to others and in truth, I'm really not sure if I am a glass half full or a glass half empty type of person. I like to think that I'm kind of a bit of both but maybe default to the glass half empty, maybe so as not to become too disappointed when people let me down (or when life, in general, doesn't go my way, which seems to be a lot).

If you have high expectations of people and of life, I think that you really set yourself up for some major hurt and disappointment. I would think that the best course of action would be to hedge your bets a little and try to stay in or around the middle, cruising somewhere between exuberant and gloomy, perhaps.

"What do you look for in a relationship, Martin?" Frances asks, keeping her eyes on the road. Deep inside me I can hear a large groan and some part of me say, "Aw, shit, here we go…"

Is this every man's experience or it just me? Why is it that I only seem to attract girlfriends that are obsessed with talking about relationship in general and the one we're in, in particular?

Guys *never* talk about relationship, except to their male buddies and that's only when the chick has fucked up or is giving him a hard time about something, usually about nothing. Most guys I know wouldn't even dare answer their girlfriend's questions about their relationship because invariably the woman that's asking has something on her mind. Her asking questions is her way of bringing up whatever problem she has with the guy, so she can let him know what she thinks needs fixing: and as far as women are concerned, just like a house, in a relationship, there's always something that needs fixing. And ten times out of ten, it's the guy's fault.

"You mean what kind of girl do I look for to be in relationship with?" I ask, knowing that that's not at all what she's asking.

"No, I mean what qualities in a relationship do you think are most important?"

"I would say honesty… loyalty and… integrity would

be on the list. Why do you ask?"

"I think it's important that two people should share a common philosophy in relationship, don't you?"

"Absolutely. Who are your favorite philosophers? Aristotle? Plato? I like Plato, he's a personal favorite." She laughs.

"I just mean that it's important that we're on the same page about things."

"I agree," I say and, hoping to put an end to this conversation, I purposefully look out the window, turning my head as if I just saw something of particular interest.

"Aren't you curious to know what I think the most important qualities in a relationship are?" Frances asks in a soft, low voice, after a long pause.

"Absolutely. I'd be very curious to know..."

"Communication," she says, emphatically. "Honest communication."

"Yes," I agree. "Honesty, integrity, loyalty and definitely honest communication. And Zen, lots of Zen."

"Be careful what you wish for," says Frances and smiles a sexy little smile.

We stop for lunch at a roadside diner but unfortunately the change of locale does not inspire a change of topic.

"I only want to have a conscious relationship with my mate from here on out," says Frances, as we receive our menus. "I'm done with..." Frances pauses, and looks like maybe she is tearing up? What is on her mind? Painful memories, perhaps? "...losers," she finishes and smiles.

"I was joking around about the whole Zen thing but obviously it's very important to you...this conscious relationship business is a Zen thing?"

"Zen encompasses everything: how you live your life and so on. When applied to a relationship between two people, it means that we practice being conscious of everything, as we go along."

"Conscious of everything?" I ask. Again, she laughs a

little.

"It sounds grandiose when I try to describe it but it basically means having an honest communication with each other, talking about the stuff no one ever wants to talk about...practicing being aware."

"Like this conversation, for instance?"

"Exactly. Let's say you're jealous but you don't say anything and instead you act out, and try to get back at me in other ways, being passive-aggressive and so on. People's feelings get hurt all the time but our tendency is to keep our pain to ourselves and then we either lash out at the world or the other person or try to bury it inside, where it festers into a cancer or something. Either way, it's unhealthy for the person and the person that they're with. Obviously the relationship suffers, if not right away, then sometime down the road as all the hurts and resentments build up to one great blow up and kaput, end of relationship."

"I see," I say, casually looking over the menu and then in my best Kung Fu grasshopper voice: "I have seen that you give this great thought. That is good, grasshopper." I thought I did a pretty good impression and considering her vintage I was sure she would get the reference but from her expression, she either didn't get it or didn't think it was funny.

"Don't take this the wrong way but are you aware that when you're uncomfortable or feeling a bit out of your depth, you make jokes?" she then asks.

Ouch.

"I like to think I make jokes to...lighten the mood, not get too serious, you know?"

"Why are you afraid of being serious? Being serious makes you feel uncomfortable? I'm not criticizing you or trying to make you feel bad and if I am, I'm sorry. But this is a perfect example of what Zen is: being aware of what you do and why you do things. What are you feeling right now? Do you want to punch me?"

"Just a little," I say, then quickly add, "I'm joking."

"Because you're uncomfortable with your feelings?"

"I guess."

"It's perfectly okay to feel like you want to punch someone, that's an instinctual human response. The feeling is a healthy one but denying it is harmful. What the Zen Buddhists would do when they had such an aggressive impulse is…or any impulse, for that matter, is acknowledge it. They would say to themselves something like, 'I'm feeling angry, in this moment, I'm feeling angry,' and in this way, by acknowledging it, the anger dissipates. Feeling angry, they didn't lash out and they didn't judge the feeling as being wrong or bad and try to bury it inside."

"I'm feeling hungry."

"Let's order. Know what you want?"

Even when the food arrives, Frances is still talking Zen. I like to think that I have an open mind but I don't think this Zen thing is for me. Trying to be 'conscious' of what I'm thinking and feeling all of the time sounds exhausting and, to be perfectly honest, extremely boring…unnatural, even.

I don't see the point to all that effort for very little purpose other than to make a relationship last longer. As far as I can tell, all relationships fail, even the married ones. It's simply a matter of time. That being said, I'm not sure if I favor ending relationships early or late. I guess it depends on how crazy you are about the girl and whether it's you or she that wants to do the terminating. If you went many years into a relationship and you're crazy about her and she does the breaking off, it's going to hurt more than if you just knew each other a little while and you weren't too into her to begin with.

Maybe I'm not understanding the whole Zen thing and should maybe give it a try. Being on the same page with someone you're in a relationship with sounds good to me. I don't think I've ever been on the same page with anyone I've ever dated, except maybe when we're lying in bed after sex, we're each a bit starry eyed and we both get the munchies together. But I don't think that's the kind of same page that she's talking about.

"We're all walking wounded, right?" Frances continues.

"Right," I answer quickly, not really sure what she means.

"When we open our hearts to someone, all our baggage comes to the surface. If the other person doesn't freak out with their own baggage also coming up, then they could really help that person to heal. As long as we don't get all reactive when one person is going through something, then each person would be there for the other. I wish we were taught all this in school."

"That and the *Kama Sutra*," I joke.

"You've read the *Kama Sutra*?"

"No. I know what it is but I haven't read it, cover to cover, no."

"Do you know what it is?"

"It's a sex manual…an old book all about sex positions. Right?"

"It's an ancient Hindu text, maybe Sanskrit, which describes human love in very poetic terms. It does include sexual positions but it's not really what one would call a manual or a how-to guide."

"That saves me a trip to Wikipedia," I instinctively joke but thank heavens, she lets it slide.

"We should go through it together. It's pretty awesome."

"I would like that."

"How's the cow?" Frances asks as I cut into my steak.

"Quit while you're ahead, Frances. A lecture on vegetarianism and I'm dating cheerleaders."

8. A NAKED PERSON CAN'T TELL LIES

When we finally get to our destination, somewhere north of San Francisco in beautiful San Rafael county, it's dark. I quickly get to meet Frances' sister, Doris and her husband, Chuck. I didn't want to ask but I think Doris is a few years younger than Frances, although Frances is so young looking, that I can't be sure. Her sister and brother-in-law seem like a very weird couple to me and, even though they're married, they don't look like they are at all in love with each other. Pretty much like most married couples, I guess.

Frances did tell me a little bit about them on the way here and I did make a note to myself never to end up like them. For starters, Doris, because of some high-paying executive job in high-end retail consulting work or something is always out of town. What kind of marriage can you be having if one of you is always traveling, right? He's a techie and works mostly at home, on the internet. I guess they Skype and phone each other to check in and see how their marriage is going from time to time.

And they do phone sex.

Which I can totally understand, considering how they are seldom together but please, phone sex? I tried it once but I just couldn't get into it. The girl I was dating lived across town and one night I called her for a booty call. Except my car was in the shop and she refused to get into hers and drive over to my place. So she suggested phone sex. It was awful. After my initial question, 'What are you wearing?' I was out of titillating questions.

"What are you wearing?"

"Nothing."

"You're not wearing anything at all?"

"No."

"Okay. Are you lying down?"

"Do you want me to be lying down?"

"It's not a hypothetical question. I'm merely trying to picture where you are in your room, if you even are in your room, are you?"

"I'm lying down on the bed, wearing nothing. Naked."

"Oh. Good. That's better. That helps."

"What would you like to do to me?"

"You know what I'd like to do to you."

"Then say it. You need to tell me. Seduce me."

"I'd like to come over and have sex with you."

"That's nice but it's not very seductive. You need to be more, I don't know, erotic."

"Have you done this many times before? I get the impression that this is not your first time." There's no way I could have my first phone sex experience with someone who is so obviously an expert. It would be like playing tennis with someone ten times better than you where you're running around the court like a madman trying just to get the ball over the net. Meanwhile, they casually stand in place, hitting the ball back with one hand and texting with the other. In one word: demoralizing.

"Is it your first time?" she asks, casually.

"Yeah. I pray to god they get my car fixed tomorrow."

"So, what would you like to do to me?"

"I don't know. What are you in the mood for?"

"I was in the mood for seduction but now I'm signing in to FaceBook."

"Oh, okay. Call you tomorrow, then."

That experience made me realize that you have to have a substantial and titillating vocabulary to master the whole phone sex thing or you will never get off the dime, or just get bogged down or worse still, become repetitive.

So Doris briefly shows Frances and me where to put our things and invites us to a home cooked supper where we all sit around the kitchen table and literally, have a feast.

"Where did you guys meet?" asks Doris.

"We met at Café Luna, my local hangout. Martin takes all his first dates there."

"That was just…" I don't get to finish.

"He struck out so many times I took pity on him."

"How did you two meet?" I ask, hoping to deflect attention away from my dating fiascos.

"We met on an internet dating site," answers Chuck, who immediately receives daggers eyes from Doris. "I'm not embarrassed," he tells her.

"What's to be embarrassed about?" asks Frances.

"It just seems so forced or desperate or something: 'how did you meet your soul mate? On GoGetASoulMateForYourself.com,' It just sounds lame," argues Doris.

"If you didn't place a listing…we never would have met, sweetheart," says Chuck.

"That's just it. I'm with you because of that listing. But I can't help thinking that maybe I've gone against fate," says Doris.

I should add here that, although I haven't personally witnessed a lot of drinking, it does appear that Doris has been imbibing for quite some time. This, I think, may explain her seemingly combatant mood, although maybe she's always like this. I don't know.

"In what way, gone against fate?" asks Frances.

"I don't know, just books I've been reading lately suggest that fate will bring you your soul mate and you need to have trust and not force things or try to do it yourself…be open to the universe and somehow, in some unexpected way, perhaps, destiny will arrange for you to bring your soul mate to you."

There's a bit of a lull in the conversation here. I think what some people are thinking, I certainly am, is that what Doris is saying is that Chuck is not her soul mate and that, by co-opting the universe and fate and stuff, she messed up her chance for destiny to bring her true partner in life. I notice that no one is raising their eyes from their food, so as not to embarrass Chuck, any more than he is, I guess.

"But don't you think that maybe you were *helping* destiny by placing that listing?" Frances says with impressive tact, "it's a bit like the story of the guy that pleads to god to help him win the lottery and after many years of pleading, god finally tells the man that he can't help him win the lottery if he doesn't buy himself a lottery ticket."

"Yeah, maybe," says Doris, without any conviction, whatsoever. "I'm going to make some coffee: everyone for coffee?"

"Let me help," says Frances and they both get up and leave me with a bereft-looking Chuck.

"How long have you guys been together?" I ask Chuck, who is now playing with the food on his plate.

"Three years," answers Chuck, "but with Doris being away most of the time, it's probably reduced to a few months."

"Long distance relationships are tough. You two have stuck with it, though. That's great," I say, waffling.

"You've been in some long term relationships?"

"No. But everyone knows that they're tough. They must be tough, not being together, in the same place, being apart…"

The dinner conversation never fully recovers, even after Doris breaks out some twelve-year-old Scotch to spice up the coffee. Chuck and Doris never say much for the rest of the evening but I can see that Frances is wired from the coffee and Scotch. Then she bores the pants off the married couple with her talk of Zen and the importance of honest communication.

To be fair to her it is a really tough crowd. They both look massively depressed and I don't even think that an impromptu visit from The Blue Man group, or something equally hilarious, would manage to cheer them up. Now, *that* is a couple in a funk.

Doris shows us to a guest bedroom which is not the one we initially put our overnight stuff in. "Tomorrow, when mum stays over, I'm going to shift you guys downstairs to the office, okay?"

When Doris leaves and closes the door, a cold chill goes up my back: Frances and I are going to sleep together. Hardly an unexpected turn of events, I did agree to come away with her for the weekend, after all. Yet strangely, now that we're finally alone, I realize that, after our previous sexual encounter, I'm actually very scared to do anything at all sexual with her.

"Take off your clothes," says Frances in a very sultry tone. I break out in a sweat and I think I might be shaking a little.

"Are you nervous?" Frances asks.

"Nervous about what?"

"I thought we were going to try honest communication?"

"I'm a little bit nervous, sure. The last time wasn't great."

"Would it help if I took off my clothes first?" Without waiting for an answer, Frances very slowly and very sexily undresses before me. Slowly unbuttoning her top, she looks at me the whole time: her breasts are full, surprisingly pert and overall, just amazing.

When she slowly and deliberately loosens her jeans belt, I feel like reaching out and stroking her boobs but I get the impression that she wants this to be a show. I don't know if it's intended but when she bends down to undo her shoes, she still doesn't break her gaze staring at me and her head is now on the same level as my crotch, which is tease personified.

Off come her jeans and, "Hello," she *totally* shops at Victoria's Secret. Her pink undies with frills and bows that scream, 'take me, I'm all yours!' When she masterfully undoes her bra and smoothly drops it to the floor, I'm so relaxed and excited at the same time that now I can't wait to join her nakedness and totally jump her bones.

I contemplate a slow, seductive striptease but I've tried it before and too many girls giggled for no apparent reason to make their reaction a one-off freak incident. I don't want to rush it with Frances, though, so undressing, I split the difference between slow and manic.

We now stand facing each other, naked and ready to go but still I display remarkable restraint and hold back. Just like Humphrey Bogart in *The Petrified Forest*, I was going to underplay the whole scene, no grandstanding performance tonight, thank you very much.

"Now you can't lie," Frances says. "A naked person can't tell lies."

"When was the last time you had sex?" I ask, coyly taking advantage of the naked-no-lying strategy. Frances simply smiles and walks closer until she is inches away. I take this as my cue to kiss her but she stops my lips with her finger.

"What do you say we let our bodies get to know each other first?"

Very gently she takes my right hand and strokes it so softly that the hairs stand erect on every other part of my body. As her fingertips slowly moves up my arms, I feel like I'm just about to burst: this woman is a total turn-on machine.

"Put your mind into the tips of your fingers and touch everything, except the obvious," Frances says with a breathy sexiness, even though I don't think she was trying to be sexy.

So, like her, I start with her hands and stroke her arms and shoulders. Her skin is so soft and silky, she feels like a porcelain doll. I've no idea why all of this is so gorgeously erotic but it is: I haven't even started on her breasts yet. As she strokes my bare chest with her delicate fingers, I'm almost shaking with desire.

"Frances?"

"Yes, Martin?"

She moves her lips just centimeters from my lips and strokes her nose softly against mine. Is that what they call an Eskimo kiss? I can feel my lower lip quivering.

"Are we going to have sex soon?"

"What do you think this is?"

"I don't know. Eskimo sex?"

"You want to fuck, is that it?"

I know she didn't intend the word 'fuck' to be exponentially, mind-blowing erotic but I'm hanging by a thread here.

"It would be good to know if that's where you intend this to end up, that's all."

"In Zen archery, the archer doesn't concern himself solely with the target. If he merges his mind with the bow, the arrow and the target, then it becomes one movement. The archer doesn't fire the arrow; the arrow shoots itself."

"That really clears things up, thank you."

"It means not to be so goal oriented." Frances is now lightly kissing my shoulders and neck. If we don't get horizontal soon, premature ejaculation is definitely in my future.

"It's the journey and not the destination."

"You do know Zen."

"I watch PBS when the porno channel gets blocked," I say, trying not to think of any porno whatsoever.

"Does this excite you?"

"The finger teasing or the running commentary?"

"Did you know that words turn women on?"

"Which is ironic: words put men to sleep."

"Then why do you have an erection?"

"The arrow has been ready to release since your bra came off."

Frances' fingers finally get introduced to my obvious parts and we finally do get horizontal and the arrow does get to fire, twice.

It was so unbelievably am-az-ing that I don't think I'll ever recover. Just as baby ducklings become imprinted by the first thing they see moving before them, I believe that sexually, I have just imprinted upon Frances. I will never make love to another woman ever again. I could but my psyche just might not be able to handle the subsequent disappointment and regret. I think I love this Zen thing. For my future survival and as a matter of maintaining my sanity, I must keep Frances…at all costs.

9. DO I LOOK OLD AND HAGGARD IN THE MORNING, SWEETHEART?

I wake early. Actually I have no idea if it's early or not, Frances is asleep beside me and it just feels early. Even if I didn't get a full eight hours sleep, I feel alive, awake and enthusiastic. Normally when I wake up before the woman I've just slept with, I'll accidently on purpose wake her up so that we can have coffee and breakfast. Or if I want to be alone, I'll sneak out of bed, get dressed, make breakfast for two and hope that after she eats, she'll toddle off home. But not this time.

Never, ever, have I woken up and felt the urge to stare at my sleeping partner. I've never had another guy admit to me that he's ever done it, either, so I just assumed that it was only something that was confined to the make-believe lovers in soppy romantic comedies.

Frances looks adorable as she sleeps, in fact, she looks like maybe what a baby looks like as it sleeps, so innocent and sweet you just feel like sighing deeply and saying, ahhhh, how cute. I'd pinch her cheeks but that might wake her.

Her eyes flutter, which I know is a sign of REM sleep and I wonder what she might be dreaming. She looks happy, so, whatever kind of dream it is, I'm sure it can't be bad. Maybe she's dreaming of me and our future together? Does she even think that way about me? That we may have a future together? Wow, I have to check myself… I'm beginning to think like a girl.

If we do have a future together, how would that work with the age difference and everything? When I'm forty, she'll be fifty-four and when she's sixty, I'll be still in my forties. What's she going to look like in ten years, when I'll be still in my prime and, like George Clooney, probably even more handsome than I am now, because fair or not, that's how it seems to work out for guys.

Maybe she'll want to get some work done on her face to make her look younger? Maybe she has had work done already; she does look very young for her age. How can you tell if someone has had work done? She does have some wrinkles, not huge, but there are some definite crow's feet around her eyes...

"Morning," says Frances, before even opening her eyes, which catches me by surprise. "You were watching me sleep?" she asks, eyes now open wide and I'm wondering how long she has been awake.

"I was waiting for you to wake up naturally, didn't want to wake you."

"I appreciate that. What were you thinking...while you were waiting?"

"I was thinking how beautiful you look."

"That's very sweet. What were you *really* thinking?"

"It's true. I was thinking how beautiful you look and..."

"And what?"

"You're looking for honest communication, right?"

"Yes, please."

"Well, suppose I say something very honest and it hurts your feelings?"

"If something you say hurts me, as long as you're not trying to hurt me, then it means that I have some unresolved issues that need healing. You'd actually be doing me a favor by pointing those areas out for me. That's how a conscious relationship is supposed to work."

"Cool. It's nothing really... I was just wondering about the future and checking out the wrinkles around your eyes and stuff."

Frances smiles, which totally relaxes me. "Do I look old and haggard in the morning, sweetheart?"

"No, not at all. Maybe down the road you will, I guess, I don't know."

"Everybody ages, Martin."

"Of course. I'm just surprised that it's not a touchy subject for you, being a woman and all."

"I didn't say it wasn't a touchy subject, sweetie, and I'd be lying to you if I said that I was okay with aging and losing my looks, it sucks rocks, are you kidding? What's the worst thing that can happen as a guy ages? He gets salt and pepper hair? Which for most guys is an improvement to their looks or big deal, you go bald, which thanks to Bruce Willis and Vin Diesel, something that used to be considered geeky is now considered sexy. So yeah, I'm majorly pissed off about the whole aging thing and the unfairness of it...how men can get away with aging and women get royally screwed."

By her tone and noticeable increase in heartbeat, I can see that Frances does indeed have a few unresolved issues around the aging thing. I have a feeling that if I ask any more questions, she will most likely go off into another tirade but I really don't want this good warm and fuzzy feeling inside to get a cold shower. Plus, I'm hungry. Maybe if we have a sexy shower together, Frances will get back in the mood.

"What are our plans for breakfast?" I ask cheerfully.

"Breakfast?" Frances says, still lost in her thoughts. "I don't know."

"I'm really liking this honest communication thing," I say, trying to pull her back.

"Yeah," she says finally, her mood shifting upwards. "Yeah, it's really important to do this. Thank you for being honest with me." She kisses me and inwardly I rejoice that she has come back. "Let's get breakfast."

Frances cooks breakfast for the four of us. Doris and Chuck are still in a depressing mood and they both look like they slept miserably, if at all. Call me a philistine but this is the first time I have had eggs Benedict. I've seen it on menus but I just never ordered it. I seemed to think that only New Yorkers or people over a certain age ordered it but I'm going to add it to my shortlist of breakfast favorites from now on, although, again, I may be disappointed with restaurant food after now being imprinted with Frances' fabulous cooking.

It is really weird sitting with Chuck and Doris. Nobody is saying anything beyond small talk and it is obvious that they really don't want to socialize, anyway. At the other end of the mood scale, Frances and I are like giddy kids that have a secret that we aren't telling anyone else. We keep catching each other's eye and smiling. It is exhilarating.

Besides Mike, it's very rare for me to communicate non-verbally with someone, especially someone of the opposite sex. Women's brains work in such fundamentally different ways, that even verbal communication with them is a challenge.

But with Frances, it's like we've been communicating non-verbally since the first time I saw her eating alone in the restaurant. I seem to know what she's thinking and she always knows what I'm thinking. It's uncanny.

After breakfast, Frances tells me that she needs to help her sister, setting everything up for her mother's birthday party. She declines my offer of help, and tells me to go out and explore the little town of Fairfax. So, camera in tow, I do.

As I walk the narrow country road to the town, I can't help but notice how absolutely beautiful everything is. The sun is radiant. It's warm but not so hot that it's uncomfortable. With my delicate skin, I don't take the sun very well. If I have to be in it, I'll usually wear a baseball cap. Here I find myself holding my face up to the sun, like it is the source of all goodness.

I don't usually notice flowers or foliage very much but today I'm struck by how pretty all the flowers are: their bright colors and varied shapes and sizes, some of them dancing in the soft breeze. Of the many, probably hundreds of thousands of photographs that I've taken in my life, I don't think I've ever taken one picture of a flower. After Still Life, Flower Photography has always been my number two on my 'most detestable uses to put a good camera to' list. It's like what schlock art is to real painting: taking pictures of flowers demeans the medium and cheapens the brand, so to speak. Amazingly, I'm zooming in X10 to get a perfect shot of the petals of a pinkish-red wild grown azalea which is stretching its adventurous little neck over a tight-knit little bunch of hydrangeas.

I need to get out of L.A. more often, I decide. Actually, I have been here a few times before, not in Fairfax exactly but in San Rafael, which is close by (Mike's parents moved up there from L.A.). It has never looked this marvelous to me before. Now I get why all the old folks describe this place as rustic and quaint. I'm not retiring any time soon, but I could definitely live here if I were.

I spend hours taking photographs of stuff that I never previously considered as photo-worthy subjects. Maybe my project direction is changing a bit and I should go with it. If someone told me a year, or even a month ago, that I'd be taking photos of flowers, bushes and hedges, mixed color ceramic tile and slate roofs, slanted wooden telegraph poles, cracked, potholed and unevenly surfaced tarmacadamed intersections and quirky local signage, I would have laughed in their face. I would probably have told them that subjects like theses were strictly for tourists, hacks and postcard photographers.

When I get back to the house, I'm pretty pooped. Some early guests have arrived. It looks like maybe they got here early to help because everybody is busy doing something to prepare for the party.

"Hi, sweetie. Have a nice walk?" Frances greets me with a tender kiss and a heart-melting smile.

"I had a great walk. Can I help with something?"

"Thanks, honey but you'll just be in the way. You look

all tuckered out, why don't you rest for a bit? Oh, I know..."
Frances takes a newly purchased book from her bag, leads
me into the front room, sits me in an armchair and hands me
the book. "I thought maybe we could try this," she half-
whispers with a hint of glee.

"*The Art Of Tantric Sex*," I read the title out loud.

"This will blow your mind," she says, again in a
conspiratorial half-whisper. "I'll go get you a drink." As she
heads off to the kitchen fridge to grab a beer and bring it
back, I'm like, jumping up and down inside, just loving this
whole grown-up relationship thing. When on earth did
Roxanne *ever* sit me down and tell me I look tired and give
me a beer and a book to read and just basically look after me
like this, in general? Uh...never.

I was always the one looking after her needs, not so
much because that's the kind of person that I am, which I
guess, I am, but mainly because the relationship was so
always about her and her telling me what her needs were.
We had more than one conversation where she seriously told
me how her needs were not getting met in the relationship.
Can anyone say, 'Prima Donna?' Looking back, I can see
how I was a total moron for putting up with it.

"Here's your beer, sweetie," Frances says with a kiss on
my head. When did Roxanne ever give me a beer and a kiss
on the head? Not once. I sigh with peace and gratitude.

As I sit reading the book on sex, I'm dimly aware that
more guests are arriving, the party is getting going and is
mainly confined to the main room, dining room and kitchen.
I don't know anybody and to be honest, because most people
attending seem to be in their sixties and seventies, I really
don't think this gathering constitutes a party, at least not
according to my definition of what a party should be. I think
one or two of them came on walkers.

Frances keeps feeding me beers and tasty appetizers and
never once gives me a hard time for sitting by myself and
not mingling. I personally hate mingling, it's even an ugly

word, and too close to the word 'mangled' to be a coincidence.

Besides, I'm finding this book about sex fascinating. Rather, I should say, it's an okay book full of really weird sexual positions, which to my mind seriously borders on porn but what I find fascinating is that Frances wants to do all these positions with me! As I look at the strange sexual positions, I find myself mentally superimposing Frances' face onto the model in the illustration. It's pretty steamy and I'm getting turned on just thinking about it.

"Are you still sitting here?" Frances asks, knowing quite well that I'm still here, she's been sneaking me beers all evening. I should probably get by now that even when she sounds earnest, she's not always being earnest, she's being jokey but I haven't gotten it down yet. I think now that she's actually being jokey.

"Best seat in the house," I playact, a secret whisper into her ear. "If I move, I'll lose it."

"Don't you want to go mingle?" she whispers back. Actually, now I'm not quite sure if she is playacting or being serious.

"Go mingle with the old people?" I say, still going with the jokey. "What do you say to old people?"

"Ask them how they feel about having wrinkles and saggy breasts."

"And what would I ask the women?" I say, holding in a smile because that was a good one.

"I don't want you talking to the women. Most of them are widows on the lookout for new husbands who still know how to drive and don't have heart conditions. Talk to Mr. Darcy over there." Although Mr. Darcy looks like he's in his eighties, he still has a sprightly demeanor and a mischievous look on his face.

"What would we talk about?"

"I don't know. Whatever guys talk about. Sports."

"What do I know about lawn bowling?" The booze

helps and I could have kept up our witty repartee for quite
some time except some geeky dude in his forties comes
through the front door, waves at Frances and off she goes to
greet him. I check him out to make sure that he has no
designs on Frances but by the way she greets him, I can see
that she has zero romantic interest in him. So I go talk to Mr.
Darcy.

"The weather is so unpredictable this year," I say,
hoping I sat by his good ear.

"When I met my wife first, that was all we talked
about."

"The weather?"

"Yes. Whether she would or whether she wouldn't!"
Mr. Darcy laughs hard but it takes me a few seconds to join
him. He may have a few years on him but those neurons are
still firing. "Whether she would or whether she wouldn't,"
he repeats himself, still laughing.

"That's funny," I say with one eye checking on Frances
who is in the kitchen still talking to the geeky dude, I think I
heard her call him, Ronald or Reinhold or something. Three
elderly women come over and sit with Mr. Darcy. Somehow
I get sandwiched in the middle, unable to escape without
climbing onto or pushing over one or two of the old ladies.

They may be old but maybe Frances is right: each of the
women do appear to be interested in Mr. Darcy. Had I not
seen the movie, Grumpy Old Men, I would have thought
flirting was only for the young but apparently the sexes
never seem to lose interest in each other. Don't know what
to think about that or maybe I'd rather not think about it. I
don't want to lose the contents of my stomach putting those
kind of images in my head.

"Suddenly you're married and you have to live with this
strange man for the rest of your life. What did we know?"
says one of the women, as I tune into their weird
conversation.

"My granddaughter asked me if she was marrying the

right man. There is no right man, I tell her. You want a pork chop or a lamb chop? Take one or the other and make the best you can out of it. The right man is the man you marry."

"It's all about sex, nowadays," another of the ladies chimes in. "They have to be sexually compatible and what have you. I was married to the same man for thirty years. We did it the same way, every time."

"I'm so glad I didn't have to do that oral sex," says one of the women, with disgust, which scores common agreement among the other women.

"He was lucky to have me lie still while he got on with it," adds another, the three ladies at this point on a roll and seemingly enjoying outdoing each other with increasing levels of lewdness.

I'm honestly not sure if they are being serious or if they are sharing a secret joke, amusing themselves by trying to embarrass me or more likely, Mr. Darcy who looks like he'd rather be with the guys, if there were a group of old guys to hang with, which sadly, there is not.

"Excuse me, ladies," I finally say, standing up. "Need to empty the bladder," which is not a lie. When I climb to the top of the stairs and turn towards the bathroom, I discover that it is a party, after all and that I found the typical party line for the solitary water closet. A shifty-looking guy in his fifties standing in front of me looks out of place and can't seem to stand still.

"The relationship I'm in, right now?" he says to me as if he knows me from way back and he's finishing the conversation we never had. "Anything I want, she'll do. Anything." I feel like asking him if he's mistaken me for his best friend from high school or maybe he's telling a joke and this is his way of mingling with strangers.

"Like what?" I ask, playing the straight guy. "What do you mean by 'anything?'"

"Anything. Kinky, S & M. role-playing, you name it. She's wild."

I'm not getting it and to make matters worse my bladder is about to explode. Is the guy being serious? "Do you find that sex games help to deepen your relationship?" I ask, with an overly serious expression.

"How do you mean?"

"That sexual games help to build up trust?" I say, now not knowing what the hell we were talking about. Who is this guy and what is he doing here?

"You don't know what I'm talking about, do you?" he asks.

"Sure," I say, at this point not giving a rat's ass about anything this freakazoid has to say, "She'll do anything." This party sucks rocks.

"Freaking wild. You'll meet her. Don't you dare steal her from me!"

What is this insane guy talking about? "I won't," I say and turn my head hoping to signal an end to the madness.

"Ever go three way?"

"Only at the track," I answer, doing my impression of Groucho Marx.

"Is that a joke? Only at the track?" he asks, looking seriously offended. He's serious about a three-way with his girlfriend? What a douche.

"I'm sorry. Are you suggesting we go..?"

"Heck, no. I wouldn't share her, are you crazy? Not with someone I just met. What if I did?"

"What?"

"You don't seem that experienced to me. Not that that's a problem. Could be to your advantage, haven't developed any bad habits."

At this point I decide to turn around to go pee in the bushes outside. A really cute twenty-five year old woman with a big smile to match her perkily erect, enormous breasts walks straight towards me, winks at me, walks right past me and kisses the weird dude on the lips.

This isn't happening, I say to myself.

"What are you two talking about?" she asks.

"Oh, guy talk," says the weirdo. "This is Martin, Frances' boy toy."

The freak knows who I am?

"Just kidding," he then adds.

"I'm Stacy," Stacy says with a flirtatious smile, extending her hand.

"Think he's cute?" asks the freak.

"Yeah, I guess," Stacy answers, another wink in my direction.

"Don't be getting any ideas," weird dude says, shaking his finger at me.

"Not me," I say, now so totally in the Twilight Zone, I wonder to myself exactly where was the threshold that I walked through that transported me into this kinky sex netherworld.

"Let's go get some more booze," Stacy says and drags the creepy guy away. I thought he wanted to go to the bathroom?

"Having fun, yet?" Frances appears.

"Who are the hep cat swingers?"

"Steve and Stacy."

"What are they doing here? Recruiting geriatrics for wild and kinky sex?"

"Steve is my ex-husband."

Wallop. Crash. Bang. You've got to be shitting me, I say to myself.

The bathroom door finally opens and it's my turn. Frances kisses me on the cheek and wisely departs. She must have seen my jaw drop and all the blood drain from my face. She was *married* to that guy? Seriously? Who *is* this woman and what am I doing here?

I've had too many beers but I still feel like drinking more. This whole geriatric party is one of the weirdest places I've been to in quite a while and that's including the all night nudist-only rave that Mike and I ended up at once (totally by accident when we got lost on the way to Joshua Tree, long story) and the all women birthday party where I struck out with every single woman in the place and couldn't figure out why until I found out it was a gathering of lesbians.

Maybe it's too soon to be meeting Frances' depressing friends, including sex-obsessed octogenarians and perverted ex-husbands. We're probably rushing things a bit. We haven't been on enough dates yet; just the two of us, where we can discover each other's dirty little secrets as we playfully laugh and giggle beneath the sheets. Then, after warm and tender Zen sex, when we were both in the place of post-coital acceptance of confessed dirty secrets, she could have told me that she has this whacko ex-husband that spiked her drink on their first date and took her to Vegas where, next thing she knows, she wakes up married.

She would then explain that she stayed married to him for fourteen years because…because he was blackmailing her or worse, he was threatening to kill her parents if she left him. He would spike her orange juice every morning, just so she would aimlessly stumble through her day and not be in any mind to go to the courts to file divorce papers. Many years went by until he met Stacy and she told him that she would do anything he wanted, so he stopped drugging Frances and finally set her free.

When I get back to the safe haven of my armchair, I'm delighted to see that it is still empty so, not knowing of any other safe place in the house to hide out in, I sink down into its nurturing bosom and turn it ever so slightly away from any possible prying eyes. If I have to talk to one more freak tonight, I'm calling a cab and I don't care if it bankrupts me, I'm heading back to L.A. tonight.

"Need help with that?" a young female voice says and when I look up, I see a totally drop dead gorgeous beauty who looks maybe around twenty years old. Hello, hello, hello, I say to myself, as if I have no internal controls, whatsoever. It isn't obvious to me that I am just staring without saying a word until she extends her hand, "I'm Janice."

"Martin," I say, shaking her soft and tender hand. "Can I get you a drink?" I say, not knowing what to say and suddenly defaulting to bar speak.

Why is it that when a guy meets a beautiful woman, his heartbeat increases, blood rushes to his face, his palms get all sweaty and if he's standing, he goes weak at the knees? There may be more symptoms, such as stammering, mental lock down, and/or amnesia and just plain old, talking nonsense but seriously, it's not just me, this happens to most guys I know, so it's got to be a biological thing, right?

Guys have no control over it, honestly. No matter how we mask it and look cool on the outside, just like a duck looks cool above water but if you look underwater at its feet, they're flapping like crazy, going like, a hundred miles an hour.

Biologically, guys respond differently to beautiful women than they do to not so beautiful women. It's a fact of life. It's nothing to be proud of and most guys hate it and wish it weren't so. Why? Because that gives a beautiful woman power over the guy. I know some guys who are powerless - literally powerless - to refuse their beautiful girlfriend anything that she wants. It's pathetic to watch and it makes men look like weak morons who deserve to be called names like pussy-whipped or worse.

I'm sure the not so beautiful women aren't crazy about it either, which is why beauty products are a multi-billion dollar industry, I guess.

As for the beautiful ones? Well, word of advice would be tread softly and wield your power with fairness and justice for all. I saw a movie trailer once that said 'Power corrupts and absolute power corrupts absolutely.' I think it was about the government and conspiracy theories but the maxim applies to everything relating to power, I think. Just something to bear in mind.

"I don't drink," says Janice. "I'm not twenty-one till August."

"Want me to spike your soda?"

"Okay."

As we casually stroll to the hard drinks table, I notice that that guy, Reinhold seems to be following Frances around like a lost puppy.

"This party blows," says Janice. "Apart from white trash Stacy over there, we're the youngest people here."

"Only in age," I say, sagely.

"What does that mean?"

"I don't know. I'm wasted."

"Want to see my short?" she asks, as I heavily spike her cola.

"Your what?"

"I'm a filmmaker. I made a short film."

"Sure. I'd love to."

Taking my hand in hers, she leads me off. "Come with me," she says softly. As the guests begin to sing, 'Happy Birthday,' Janice and I enter the office off the hall which has a TV and a DVD player. Sitting me down on a sofa, she puts in her DVD and switches off the room light. I'm beginning to feel a little uncomfortable with the intimacy and I'm really not sure if I am doing something wrong, sneaking off from the main party.

"What kind of movies do you make?" I ask, in a neutral tone which I hope suggests that I'm only here because of my interest in student film work and art, in general. But, as the movie starts, she doesn't answer and sits beside me on the sofa.

I feel like saying that I'm here with Frances to clarify my position, but then she might think that it is presumptuous of me to think that she is interested in me. She'd probably laugh and later ridicule me in front of other guests and, as a consequence, it would embarrass the heck out of Frances. I don't want to risk that or come off looking like an idiot, so I don't say anything.

I figure that she's probably just bored at an old folks' party and maybe she wants or needs some encouragement of her work, her passion and her art, from an objective observer.

As classical music plays in the background, the camera slowly pans across a four poster bed. In the scene, Janice lies dressed in period attire and looks bored. A moment later, she gets up and looks out the window. She sees a gardener, chopping wood.

Janice beckons to the gardener and he tosses aside his axe, wiping the sweat from his brow, which to some ladies might be perceived as a turn on. The gardener sheepishly enters the room where Janice is and stands like he's awaiting further instructions. Janice approaches him and takes off his hat: his long flowing hair falls down. The gardener is a woman.

Is this going where I think it's going? Is this a friggin' porno film?

I sneak a look at Janice but she seems riveted, as if watching it for the first time. On screen Janice takes the gardener's hand and places it on one of her heaving, full breasts. Leaving it there, Janice slowly undresses the shy, female gardener.

I have absolutely no idea why guys get turned on watching girl-on-girl action. On so many levels it doesn't make any sense why guys find it so terribly hot but they do and, guess what? I'm no exception. I'm beginning to panic because I have no friggin' idea of how to watch this and in the process, prevent myself from getting a boner.

Short of closing my eyes and thinking of something horrible like the holocaust or something, I don't think it can be done. Okay, if I make some excuse to leave, will that be like saying to a neophyte filmmaker that her work sucks? If I stay and this goes where I think it's going, am I watching porn with a young woman I'm attracted to at a party my girlfriend brought me to and I can't stop myself from getting turned on? This is so effed up.

"Are you liking it?" Janice asks, interrupting my thoughts.

"So far," I say, tactfully. "What would you call this, soft porn?"

"It's erotica," Janice says, with a tone in her voice as if she's insulted.

"What's the difference?" I ask, because I seriously don't know.

"Don't you see the parallels with D. H. Lawrence?"

"I'm not familiar with his work. What kind of films does he make?"

"The author, D. H. Lawrence," she corrects me, "*Lady Chatterley's Lover*?"

"I haven't read it, sorry."

"It's like if Mrs. Lawrence was to write the book, instead of her husband, maybe this is what it would look like," she says earnestly.

I have no idea what point she's making with this erotica movie, except maybe she's making some feminist point about how men objectify women. I guess she's turning the tables…and now, instead of a man, it's a woman that's objectifying women? That doesn't make any sense. I need to get out of here fast and get another drink.

On screen, the door suddenly opens and the women react with panic as, I assume it's the husband, comes barging in. He checks out the women and after a long cinematic moment that is loaded with all kinds of meaningful looks to each other, presumably denoting some weird shit subtext that I'm not even going to try to decipher, the Janice character extends her hand to the husband and invites him to join them.

He smiles as if he likes the idea and then he starts to undress and, oh, come on, this is porn, I don't care what bullshit feminist point she claims to be making.

"You hate it," Janice says, biting her lower lip. Boy, is it hot in here or is it just me?

"No, not at all," I unabashedly lie. "I think it has a great message."

The door opens and Frances stands in the doorway.

"There you are," she says to me. "What are you up to?"

"Nothing," I automatically say, in exactly the same tone and reactive sense of guilt with which I answered my father, when I was thirteen and he caught me smoking pot round back of the house.

"I'm showing Martin my short," Janice says with a mix of familiarity and coldness that I can't quite decipher. She pauses the DVD with the remote. "You don't have a problem with me entertaining your boyfriend, do you?" Okay, definite coldness there. How come everyone here knows who I am?

"Are you being entertained, Martin?" Frances asks and I can't tell if she's okay with everything or if I'm in trouble.

"Oh, sure," I say, as neutral as I can.

"Steve is about to leave, if you want a ride," Frances says to Janice. "Or you're welcome to crash here."

"If I stay here, you'll make me help clean up tomorrow," Janice answers, getting up. "I'll go with Steve." She then turns to me. "Take care of the DVD for me and I'll pick it up tomorrow, okay? We can talk about it then."

"You bet."

Janice leaves and Frances opens the door more fully to see what's on the screen: a threesome. "You don't have to watch the rest," she says.

"Are you guys related?"

"Janice is my daughter. Beautiful, isn't she?"

"You never said you had a twenty-year-old daughter?"

"You said you wanted things to be revealed as we went along, right? You can ask me anything you want."

"Steve is her father?"

"No. I never kept in touch with her father. I was very

young when I had her."

"You were married twice?"

Frances sits beside me and takes my hands in hers. "I got pregnant when I was eighteen. It was all about free love back then and…well, I wasn't sure who the real father was. Steve was crazy about me. He was older and, at the time, I thought he was really cool and very gallant for wanting to marry me when I was carrying someone else's child. But that didn't work out, obviously. As time went by we both realized that we weren't very compatible but we remained friends and he was like a father to Janice. I know you think he's weird and he is but I understand his weirdness and I know his heart. He has been a good friend to me over the years. There you have it."

"You married again?"

"Yes, I did marry someone since Steve but that didn't end well, at least for me and I don't want to have any contact, ever. Let's save that story for another day, what do you think?"

"This is a lot to digest and I honestly don't know what to think."

"Welcome to my life." She smiles and once again, melts my heart and brings a smile to my lips. She is truly lovely and I feel giddy that she seems to really like me.

"We're sleeping in here tonight. There's some sheets and blankets behind the sofa, okay? Enjoy the movie." She gives me a big wink and closes the door behind her as she leaves. I stare blankly at the TV for a few moments, not sure of my thoughts. There's no way I can watch the rest of this crap. What I really need is another drink. Or six.

10. TANTRIC SEX

Okay, curiosity gets the better of me and I do watch the rest of Janice's short. Just like any porn I've ever watched, which is not a lot, after the first titillating ten minutes, it becomes repetitive and boring. I'm really trying not to focus on the erotic aspect but instead look at it from a political point of view. I still don't get it.

She can call it anything she likes: a satire, a political indictment, a commentary, an homage, a revisionist portrayal…Two women and a guy getting it on in a four poster bed? It's porn.

At some point, I must have dozed off and I've no idea what time it is now. The "short" film has ended and the DVD logo floats around on the TV screen. Everything sounds quiet outside and there's no sign of Frances. Is she punishing me by sleeping somewhere else?

I look behind the sofa and try and make a bed out of the jumble of blankets and sheets that I find there. It's dark, the light switch is on the wall by the door and I'm too lazy to walk over and switch the lights on. I don't think I can take the glare of the main lights, anyway, so I just drop where I am and try to get cozy among the wad of messed up blankets and bedding.

The door opens quietly and I smile that Frances is going to sleep with me after all. Except it doesn't sound like Frances. The walking sounds like a man. I sneak a peek from around the end of the sofa and see a man's pair of shoes. I hear him pick up the phone and dial.

"Hello there, my hot little Chickadee," he says. It sounds like Chuck; who is he calling at this hour? Should I let him know that I'm here? "Guess who?" he says and his voice is really flirty. Maybe I should innocently cough or something.

"Boy, am I feeling horny for you, my hot little pumpkin." Holy shit. I think now that the cat is out of the bag and if I were to declare myself it would be obvious that I have just caught him *cheating on his wife!*

"I want to ram my rod into your hot lower lips, you make me so hard."

Oh, please god, let this not be happening. Phone sex? Seriously?

"I'm a horny, horny ramrod and I want you so bad I'm going to…"

Okay, at this point I cover my ears and mentally sing the last song that I heard, whatever is easily accessible. I sing 'Happy Birthday to You' as long and as loud as I can until my inner eardrums can't take any more volume. The entire time I keep an eye on the door, praying that this horror of all horrors will be over soon and that the cheating son of a gun creeps back to his unassuming missus.

After what seems like an eternity, the door finally opens and Chuck sneaks out the same way he skulked in: like a thief in the night. Except this is his house and I guess he can do what he likes but jeez…

I'm numb from shock and the cold and feeling lost and alone in a strange room in a strange house, I gather up the bedding and huddle on the couch, practically rocking myself to and fro to stay calm. Frances finally comes in. I'm so glad to see her, I rush up and hug the life out of her.

"Wow," she says, happily. "Somebody missed me."

"Oh, I missed you," I almost sob. "Don't ever leave me again," and in this moment I truly mean it.

"What's going on?"

"What's going on?" I ask, with all the grandiose indignation I can muster. "All your friends are weirdness personified: your ex-husband is a pervert, your daughter is a pornographer and your sister's husband is having an affair."

"Chuck is having an affair?"

"I would have taped the conversation but it was so disgusting, even my cell phone had its ears covered."

"What was disgusting? What are you talking about?"

"I'm lying asleep behind the sofa and in sneaks Chuck, like…like a thief in the night…he didn't know I was here and he got on the phone and called *his mistress*."

"I don't believe you. If he did call someone, it could have been a client or something."

"Trust me. Whatever *client* takes calls at this time of night and has a conversation like that is in only one kind of business. It may be the oldest profession but it's not a business you'd declare on your end of year taxes, if you get my drift."

Frances looks at me like I'm nuts. So I pick up the phone that Chuck used.

"Don't believe me, hit redial. See who answers. If you get her machine, you've got a name and a number. Case closed."

"What if it's not a she?"

"Pretty sure it's a she. Go on. I dare you."

"Did he say a name? Did you get his lover's name?"

"No. But apparently she answers to the name of 'hot little chickadee.'"

I didn't actually think that Frances would do it but she does press redial and holds the phone to her ear. "Hello, who is this, please?" says Frances. I'm standing with my hands on my hips, and as I await vindication, I can't help but admire how brave this woman is. If she was a man, I'd be admiring her *hueovos* but I'm not sure if you can use that term for a woman, even though, technically they do have them, at least once a month for some and…

"Oh, hi, Doris. It's Frances." What, now?

"I know it's late but I…we can't find the pillows." Frances listens and then hangs up. We look at each other for a long moment, just the way Watson and Sherlock Holmes do on that TV show when they're trying really hard to crack a difficult case.

"Chuck called his wife from the downstairs phone to have phone sex?" I say, encapsulating the mystery.

"I guess. If that's what you heard."

"I know what I heard," I say. "I'm no expert in the field but I know phone sex when I hear it."

"Maybe, because they are apart so much…" Frances says and stops.

"That that's the only way they can have sex?" I finish her thought. "On the phone?"

"At least he's not having an affair, right?"

"Yeah," I agree. "It may be weird but at least no one's getting hurt. Except maybe my poor ear drums and my delicate psyche."

"Well, why don't you get your delicate psyche over here to bed and I'll kiss your ear drums better."

"Okay."

I lie down and take Frances into my arms. She smells so…soft and, well, I don't know…fragrant. Whatever it is about her scent, I just want to lose myself in her…beingness, for want of a better word.

"What did you think of the book?" she whispers into my ear. I instantly grin. Holy crap, she wants to have tantric sex.

"I liked it," I say, which is a ridiculous understatement.

"What did you like about it?" she whispers playfully, her lips brushing against my ear lobes and inextricably registering in the pleasure centers of my brain.

"I like…trying new things."

"You want to try new things with me?"

"Totally."

"What was your favorite…position?"

"All of them. There wasn't a position in there that I didn't like. I want to do all of them…with you." I almost giggle.

"Why don't we start at the beginning?"

"Absolutely. Now?"

"No time like the present, right? Unless you're too tired."

"I'm not too tired. Are you too tired?"

"Take your clothes off."

I can't explain how fantastically gorgeous it is to feel Frances' naked body against mine: her warm soft skin is unreal. If I was a poet I'd be using words like yielding and yearning and, I don't know, mellifluous, which would be a huge challenge to put into an acceptable sentence. She yielded her mellifluous body into my yearning embrace. Not actually sure what mellifluous means but then I never understood half the poetry that I learned by heart in high school.

"Now lean back a little," Frances says softly as I effortlessly get into position, "does that feel good?" It feels so gosh darn good, that I now know where songwriters get their song lyrics from. We are moving, slipping and sliding, grooving rhythmically to the beat of each other's bodies. Ooh, baby, baby, it's a wild world...

"Does that feel good?" Frances asks again.

"Oh, yeah."

"Feels good for me, too."

"It's more than good, it's amazing," I say, just as I'm about to...

"Don't come," she says.

"What?"

"Don't come. It's tantric. You read the book, right?"

"The text was so boring and confusing, I mostly just looked at the pictures."

"In tantric sex you reach orgasm without coming."

"What, now? Isn't that an oxymoron?"

"You circulate the energy internally, instead of letting it explode in orgasm."

"Too late," I say and I explode. I see stars. I see galaxies forming and exploding and like a circle in a spiral and wheel within a wheel, never ending or beginning…

"Are you okay?" Frances asks as I collapse to the bed.

"I'm fine," I say with the widest grin my face has ever seen. "How are you?"

11. LOVE IS A DRUG

I wake up before Frances and again, all I want to do is watch this beauty sleep. I've never watched anybody sleep before. I've seen people asleep but it's not the same, I've never actually studied them. Not that I'm studying Frances so much as just admiring her, maybe admiring is not the right word, either. I can see how poets have difficulty finding the right words to define things that aren't really definable.

Maybe I will try my hand at poetry and try to describe what I'm seeing with my eyes when I take a picture of something. I really think that photography is like poetry for the eyes.

She sleeps like an infant sleeps
This lady with the turbulent past
Yet in sleep, innocence becomes her

"You watching me sleep again?" Frances says without opening her eyes.

"You're beautiful," I say.

"Sounds like you got it bad."

"I got it bad and that ain't good," I say, without missing a beat. "Got what bad?"

"When a person falls in love, the body releases a bunch of chemicals and hormones. You're high on endorphins."

"What are you saying? Love is a drug?"

"Yep."

"I don't care. I'm feeling good."

"You'd do anything for me, right now, wouldn't you?"

"You have something in mind?" I say suggestively.

"Breakfast in bed would be a real treat," Frances says, bursting my bubble, that's not what I had in mind, at all.

"You got it!" I say, jumping up instantly because, in

truth, all I want to do is make her happy.

The kitchen looks like every other kitchen the night after a party: empty beer and wine bottles, half-empty glasses, dirty dishes…it's a mess. The fridge is still stuffed with food not served and plenty of leftovers but who wants to eat heated up *hors d'oeuvres* for breakfast?

I do what I usually do when I'm hungry but don't know what to eat: hold open the refrigerator door and stare at what's in there, imagining combos in my head: hm, pigs in a blanket with cocktail sausages and shrimp? I don't think so. Besides, I think Frances is a vegetarian, so I'll play it safe and make some eggs. Are eggs vegetarian?

"Help you find something?" says a voice and I turn and it's Chuck, dressed in a robe.

"Eggs," I manage to say.

"Yeah, me too," he says "Sent down to make eggs for the missus. Want to join forces?"

"Sure."

It helps that Chuck knows where everything is but it doesn't help that I can't get last night's phone dialogue out of my head: making eggs for the hot little chickadee, I sing-song to myself like I have no internal discipline.

"Does Frances like hot spices in her eggs?"

"Yeah, I guess. Who doesn't, right? Eggs and hot spices, oh yeah," I babble, mindlessly, feeling beyond awkward.

"You want to start the toast?" he asks.

"Toast, yes. Toast and eggs, goes together like…" I can't think of anything, so I stop mid-sentence. I can feel him looking at me out the corner of his eye. He thinks I'm weird. Which is what the kettle does, says a voice inside, calls the pot black or maybe it's the pot that calls the kettle black, either way…He thinks I'm weird? He's weird.

"How's the toast coming?" he asks, knowing that the toast is not coming along so well considering that I can't find the bread or the toaster. "The bread is in a bread bin behind the juicer and we use the toaster oven on the top left shelf," he says and, for some reason, I can't help thinking that he's judging me as an idiot. Or maybe I'm just feeling antagonistic towards him, like we rub each other the wrong way. I've no idea why, but sometimes two people simply don't like each other.

"I really need that toast," he says. "The eggs are almost done."

Why doesn't he come out and say, 'how hard can it be to make toast, moron?' because that's the way he's sounding.

"Why don't you keep an eyes on these and I'll start the toast," he says. "I know my way around. It is my kitchen, after all." He smiles but I can see right through him. He's not fooling anyone with that fake smile.

"Good morning, Martin," Doris stands in the doorway, also in a robe.

"Morning."

"Honey," she says to Chuck, "I'll be in with Frances. We can all eat together."

"Okay," says Chuck and when he turns, she has left. "In with Frances where?" he says to me. "Where did you two guys sleep?"

"In the office," I say smartly and promptly turn to go to the bathroom. When a plate drops and crashes on the floor, I don't turn back to look.

Like a slumber party for adults, the four of us sit on the floor of the office eating toast and eggs. Chuck and I never say a word throughout the entire meal, in fact he can't even look at me, nor I at him. Our lack of participation isn't even noticed, as Doris and Frances talk the whole time. I guess they need to catch up about stuff: their jobs, their mother and so on.

I get the impression that they don't talk much to each other, except maybe around holidays. Probably because Doris is on the road so much, that would make sense.

Seriously, that woman needs to get a different job, closer to home or just plain home. How long can their marriage last like this? It's obviously not my place to say but, come on, if the only way you can make love to your husband is on the phone, an idiot could tell you that it's a problem.

After breakfast I finally get Frances all to myself. So we walk into Fairfax to window shop and hang out at a coffee shop. There aren't many windows to window shop, I count six in total and not one is of any interest to me, mostly women's fashion, antiques and a bunch of restaurants. I don't care. I am with Frances and we are walking hand in hand, actually it is more meandering than walking.

And I know that she is enjoying it too. I can see it in her eyes, she is so relaxed and has a smile on her face the entire time. We don't talk about our relationship or Zen or even about relationships of the past, thank heavens. It is more, 'Oh, look at that,' when she sees something she likes or 'Oh, that's cute,' when she notices a nice house or a pretty garden or something.

I am enjoying her company so much that I don't stop even once to take a photograph. It is like I don't want to let go her hand; her soft, tender hand that seems to fit perfectly into mine, just the way our bodies fit perfectly into each other at night.

I love how she keeps telling me that whatever it is I'm doing, just normal, everyday stuff, is cute. Nobody has ever told me before that the ordinary stuff that I do, all the time, is cute. Like the way I hold the coffee mug, not by the handle but sort of grab the entire mug in my hand and drink away from the handle…apparently, that's cute. I've been doing that all of my life. Or the way I kind of bite my lower lip when I'm thinking hard, that is also cute. Even the way I put a sweater on, in one fell swoop, she finds that cute, too. I play it down and tell her that it's just the way I've always been doing things but secretly, I'm loving it. It makes me feel like she really likes me, that I'm special to her. I want her to like me.

Even though we spent a few hours together, it feels like a brief moment and before I know it, we have to get back to get ready for dinner. She has arranged for us to meet Steve and Stacy for a meal in a restaurant somewhere and I as much as I am dreading it, I figure that whatever baggage comes with this delightful woman, it is okay by me. I'll just have to get used to it. She'll have to meet my friends at some point and I've no idea how she'll react going out with Mike and Gloria to Frankey's for Fear Factor Karaoke or Puke Poetry Slam night. The nicer I am in her world, the more open and accepting that I can be, well, I'm hoping that it will help to offset whatever second thoughts she might have when she enters my own peculiar world.

In theory, I'm down with accepting whatever baggage Frances comes with but, as I'm checking out the menu in some pretentious, over-priced, fake-French restaurant, sharing a table with Frances, Steve, Stacy and Janice, I can't help but think how weird this whole escapade is.

I'm sitting with my girlfriend beside her ex, who's old enough to be my father. Across the table is my girlfriend's daughter who's just about in the age range of the women that I would like to date and beside her is Stacy, who is the same age as me and dating someone probably older than her father. And, oh, yeah, they're all freaks.

"What did you think of my short, Martin?" Janice asks.

"Excellent."

"No, really. No bullshit. What did you think?"

"I thought it may have been a little bit, kinda verging on the pornographic."

"But didn't you get the politics?"

"The politics?"

"That in this version, the wife, the woman is in control."

"And she's a lesbian," adds Stacy.

"Bisexual, actually," corrects Janice.

"D. H. Lawrence's wife wasn't bisexual," counters

Stacy.

"So?" retorts Janice, "Virginia Woolf was married to a guy. She was a lesbian. Duh."

"She didn't write about sex."

"So?"

"She probably wasn't getting any," jokes Steve because, let's face it, all he does is joke. I have no idea what anyone is talking about here. Except the one thing I do catch is that these people don't like each other very much.

"Your short film rocks!" I say to Janice in a tone that I hope will end this segment of the conversation. I'm in favor of focusing on the menus, so that we can order some food and get the heck out of here.

"Thank you, Martin," Janice says, probably for the same reason.

I decide that I am just going to bury my head in the menu and for the rest of the evening say as little as possible and just let them go ahead and bite each other's heads off with their sharp tongues.

The menu is really pissing me off too: I hate pretentious places like this where everything's in French, as if that makes it taste better, with very minimal translations into English and then when you ask, the snobby waiter treats you like a philistine, 'what, you don't understand French? Mon Dieu! you are so ignorant'

So, in between Janice's criticism of her mother, and Stacy and Janice's nasty barb exchanges, not to mention, Steve's contributions (which is to get the odd joke in, here and there, which *always* has some perverted double meaning), I'm starting to wonder more and more about Frances.

If it's true that people judge people based on the friends that they keep and a person is guilty by association, then where does that leave Frances? What kind of person is she, really? I know so little about her. Granted, she's related by blood in some cases but look at all these freaks and crackpots she hangs out with. What if she herself is a crazy person with multiple personalities and the nice person that I get to hang out is but one of many other nutcase personalities that she keeps hidden from my view?

Even if I am overreacting, and she is basically a kind and decent person, what is she doing with me? Why does she want a relationship with a guy that's fourteen years her junior? And why has it taken me so long to start asking these questions? Like Steve said the other evening, does she see me as some kind of boy toy? Why isn't she in relationship with a guy her own age? Actually, why isn't she in a relationship, period?

All of a sudden I'm beginning to see things more clearly. This is just a little fling for her. I'm someone that Frances can amuse herself with in between her serious relationships. I don't think that she's taken me seriously since the first time we went out on a date together. I should have known that I was just an entertainment to her, especially when she joked about her first love being some dog next door, what was that about?

What about all this talk about Zen and honest communication and the way that she wants to be in control all of the time? Maybe she can't hack it in a grownup relationship, and I'm a perfect candidate because she thinks I'm dumb and I won't question or challenge her about anything that she says. She's going to play with me like a cat plays with a mouse and then toss me aside when some Tomcat arrives on the scene and then it's see you later, grasshopper.

"What are you thinking?" she asks as we drive back to L.A. in her fancy car, that she's driving.

"I can't believe that you have a twenty-year-old daughter and that you were married to that guy Steve and then you were married again to some mysterious dude, whose name you don't even dare mention."

"Okay," she says, and I can hear her thinking, 'where

did this all come from and what do I say to pacify him.' "Do you want to talk about it?"

"What's to talk about?" I say and I don't care if I'm sounding pissy.

"I was young and foolish, what can I say?"

"What are you doing with me?" I ask, "what is this, you and me? Why are you dating someone so young, I mean, comparatively young?"

"I'm not dating you because you're young, Martin. I'm dating you because I like you."

"I think you're dating me because... I don't know why you're dating me. I don't think you're taking this seriously...taking me seriously at all. It's like you're just, I don't know, biding your time till something better comes along."

When Frances pulls to the side of the road and stops the car, it feels like somehow the roles have suddenly become reversed and she's the guy and I'm the hormonally challenged girlfriend that's throwing a hissy fit, all needy and vulnerable and shit. She looks me straight in the eyes.

"Of course I take you seriously. I take you very seriously. I wouldn't have invited you to meet my family if I wasn't serious about you. I don't take boyfriends to visit my family, Martin. I didn't say anything but taking you home was a big deal for me."

"I didn't know that," I say, sheepishly. "I didn't know it was a big deal."

"It was a very big deal." She puts her hand on my cheek. "I'm not playing with you, sweetie, if that's what you're worried about. I like you a whole lot."

"You do?" I say, now feeling a lot better.

"Yes, I do. Which is why I wanted to invite you to a relationship seminar that's starting next week." She reaches into the glove box and hands me a brochure: 'The Relationship Seminar You Can't Afford To Miss.' "What do you think?"

"A relationship seminar? Seriously? Isn't that just for morons?"

"You've got nothing to learn?"

"I learn as I go. Like most people."

"Sometimes it helps to know beforehand what to expect, don't you think? It's like, if you knew there was a mountain up ahead, you could bring some supplies, some rope or something."

"If you knew there was mountain in the way, you'd stay home and watch TV and maybe watch someone else climb it on the Discovery Channel or something. I don't know what we're talking about."

"I got pregnant at eighteen, married at twenty. I don't regret having Janice but I sure as heck would have preferred to have had that parental talk before I left the house."

"So, what you're saying is that you don't want to leap until you know what it is that you're leaping into? I mean with all the books you read and these seminars and stuff…you're trying to…minimize your risk?"

"I'm trying to learn. I'm trying to have better, more successful relationships…to understand better and not keep fucking up one relationship after another. Do you have the relationship thing all worked out? There's nothing you need to learn or understand better?"

"Can I ask you a question?"

"Sure."

"Do you want to have a successful relationship with me?"

"I think that's what I just said, Martin. Yes."

"You want to be in love with me and be loved by me?"

"Again, yes."

"Well, then we're arguing about the same thing, except you think we have to read books and go to seminars and stuff, when all we have to do is, just do it!"

"Do what?"

"Fall in love."

"Is that what you want, Martin? You want to fall in love with me? You want us to fall in love?"

"I'll tell you exactly what I want. I want to feel the joy and the mystery and the passion of being in love. I want to stare into my lover's eyes for hours and hours. I want to feel her skin against mine and caress it like it was the most precious thing in the world. I want to go somewhere I've never been before, somewhere so new, it's going to blow my mind." I took France's hands in mine. "I would love to go there with you, Frances."

"That's so beautiful, Martin."

"Thank you."

"But I'm not your happiness. And you're not mine. What you're describing, you have to find within yourself or in your work or something."

"What?" That was not the response I was expecting and against my better judgment, I stare at her for too long a moment with my mouth half open.

12. FALLING IN LOVE AGAIN

Feeling deflated, confused and uncertain of the whole relationship thing, I'm done talking, so we hit the road again and both remain silent for what seems like an eternity. I really don't know what her problem is. It's almost as if every time we have the chance of having a romantic moment, she throws a bucket of cold water all over it and it pisses me off. Why be in relationship if you don't want to be in love? It doesn't make any sense. I mean, if you're dating and having sex and stuff, isn't it a given that falling in love is part of the package?

Unless, of course, you agree that you're just fuck buddies and everyone then knows that falling in love is not part of that arrangement. But we never agreed to that, unless it is for her but she just neglected to tell me. So maybe I am her boy toy, after all.

But then there's the whole taking me up to meet her family thing, which is one thing fuck buddies do not do but then again, maybe she didn't want to face her crazy family alone and she brought me up as some kind of support or maybe to create a distraction or something.

Another thing that fuck buddies do not do is that whole Zen sex thing with the putting your mind in your hands and being present to every friggin' sensation in your body and having foreplay for like an hour before anything really happens. And what about the tantric sex thing where you 'circulate energy' but you don't actually fuck; fuck buddies definitely don't do that.

"I guess I'm just scared," Frances finally says, breaking the deafening silence. "I can blame all the ex-husbands and ex-boyfriends that I want but I really haven't been very good at relationship. It's been one train wreck after another. I must really suck at relationship."

Even though Frances smiles, I can see that it isn't a real smile that comes from the heart and is more a smile of masked hurt. Although Frances is the first to break the silence with some kind of admission, and probably most people would welcome such a moment, but to be honest, I dread these heart to hearts, especially with a woman because I have no idea what the right things to say is.

"If I could give up on relationship altogether and be happy, I would, but I know that I wouldn't be happy alone, just by myself. I do want what you want, I do, I'm just...terrified," and the more she continues, all heart-felt and deep and obviously hurting from some past pain, the more I squirm inside: what do I say?

"Maybe you shouldn't be so hard on yourself," I say. "I think most people are scared inside."

"Are you, Martin? Do you feel scared inside?"

"No. I don't think so." One of us has to stay strong.

"And you really want to be in love with me?" says Frances, brightening. Is she considering it?

"Yes. Yes, I do."

"You want to stare at me while I sleep and...run through the poppy fields playing catch and kiss and have mad passionate sex in every room and every nook and cranny of the house."

"All of the above, yes!"

"Then let's do it," declares Frances. "Let's fall in love!"

"Just like that?" I ask.

"Just like that!"

"I'm excited but to be honest, I didn't know that falling in love was a decision we need to make."

"To adopt the Zen mind is to be conscious of everything you do. That includes falling in love," she responds, now sounding like she's back to her reasonable, Zen self persona.

"In every room and every nook and cranny, I like it!"

"I've got a few days before I start my next project. Let's

spend some serious time together, just you and me. Let's be carefree and silly, what do you say?" she asks cheerfully.

"Okay!"

"And next weekend we'll do the relationship seminar. Deal?"

"Deal." Had she asked for all my pay for the coming year and the pink slip to my car, I would have given it to her. Anything to end this conversation and get back to being happy with each other.

The next few days are the most incredible, wondrous and magical days I've ever spent in a romantic relationship in my life. If some wizard had given me a magic wand and said, 'Here, go ahead and wish for whatever it is you want to wish for,' spending these amazing days and nights with Frances would have been my wish.

I remember when I was a kid, in order to feel close to my parents, I'd watch grown-up movies on TV with them. For the most part they were boring, but they would always have these glorious montages of love scenes where the guy and the gal would run through tall grass and wild flowers in the sun or they would run on the beach together and splash each other in the surf.

The couple in love, in the movie, would picnic together on a grass knoll by the river's edge and they would playfully feed each other grapes or strawberries or, I guess, whatever love berry was in season.

Frances and I do them all.

We have dinner on a rooftop with twinkle lights and champagne in a bucket. We lie in the sand in each other's embrace at moonlight just as the surf came crashing into us, just like Deborah Kerr and Burt Lancaster in *From Here to Eternity*.

We ride the Ferris wheel at night on Santa Monica pier and I shoot three ducks with an air gun and win her a fuzzy, cute teddy bear. We walk hand in hand and share a soft ice cream cone. It melts in the sun and runs down my fingers but

Frances quickly licks them and then she laughs. I tickle her and she laughs some more and then she runs and I chase her and I catch her and we both laugh and then we kiss deeply.

And, true to her word, we have lots of sex. We have sex in the shower and sex on the stairs and sex on the sofa and on the kitchen table and her writing desk and in the hallway and out back in the bushes when it is dark and we have to be so quiet but it is hard to have sex outside, half-standing up and we giggle because it is just so darn daring and outrageous.

And then I tell her that I love her.

I massage her foot and surrounded by pillows, candles, soft lighting, romantic music and lying post coital on the sheepskin rug in front of a smoldering fire, I can feel her instantly tense up. Which probably should be an indication for me not to say anything more, but I really feel full of love right now and I want to share my feelings.

"All I've ever imagined that I could have from a girlfriend is to be understood. That she'd know me. Not the little things like my favorite color or something but that she could really see me for who I am. I feel like I have all that with you."

Frances pulls her foot away and embraces her knees to her chest, which I take not to be a great sign. "I bumped into an old friend of mine on the street the other day, some guy I used to work with," she says in a kind of neutral tone. "He asked me how I was. 'Great,' I said, 'just great.' Then he asked me if I had broken up with my boyfriend, which I thought was a weird question to ask, so I asked him, why ask that question? And he says, oh, it was always the boyfriend with you. If he's happy, you're happy and when he's sad, you're sad…"

Frances looks at me with what looks like deep sadness in her eyes. "I don't want to be that person anymore," she says.

"What person? I'm not sure I know what you're talking

about."

Before Frances gets a chance to answer, there's a knock at the front door.

"Are you expecting someone?" I ask.

Taking a look through the peephole, "It's Ronald," she says and just as I'm saying, "You're letting him in?" she opens the door to let him in. As she does so, sharp sunlight comes blasting through, as, even though it's almost a hundred degrees Fahrenheit outside, in order to have the coziness of the fire, we cranked up the air conditioner.

"Wow, it's dark in here," Ronald says as he kisses Frances on the cheek. "You've got a fire going? It's nearly triple digits out there."

Amazingly, not once does he look at me or acknowledge my presence. In fact, the whole time, he acts like I'm not even here.

"Sorry for showing up like this," he says, not sounding one bit sorry. "But I've left you like six messages on your voicemail and the client's seriously freaking about the changes."

"What changes?" asks Frances.

"Yeah, that was voicemail message number one. They want some major changes to your design. I brought over the blueprints." As Frances takes the blueprints to her desk and turns on the bright lights, I'm wondering just what has happened. One minute we're talking love and exchanging sweet nothings and the next it's Grand Central Station in here?

"I'll put on some coffee," Frances says. "Want some coffee?" she asks Ronald, the puppy dog from the party.

"Absolument," he says with a phony French accent. Really pissed that I'm being totally ignored, not just by Ronald Reinhold, a complete dick, which I can take, but particularly by Frances, especially as I had just a second ago bared my soul to her and put my feelings about her out there...I decide to go.

I want to get the heck out of here and not come back. In fact, my absence obviously won't even be missed. So I go to the bedroom and quickly dress. Just as I'm putting my shoes on, Frances comes in.

"Martin, I'm so sorry, I have to deal with this. It's work, okay?"

"You didn't even introduce us," I say angrily. "This is the guy that was stalking you all night at your mom's birthday party. That's how badly he wants to get into your pants."

"Ronald's an old friend. He got me this job."

"Whatever."

"Martin, the past few days have been real fun but we can't cocoon ourselves away from the world and live in some little love bubble forever. I have to deal with this, okay?"

"Yeah, well, guess what? I think our little love bubble just burst," and with these parting words, I grab my overnight bag and I'm out of here.

13. HELLO MOM

When I get to my car, I'm not too surprised to find a parking ticket on the windshield. The car's been sitting here for days and who pays attention to a sign that says street cleaning on Friday, when you're parking there on Tuesday? Besides, this is Santa Monica, pretty much famous for issuing parking tickets on the slightest pretense, like maybe if your car is green, they are allowed to ticket it on whatever day they pick up the recyclables and double the fee on International Earth Day.

I open the door and angrily fling my bag across the passenger seat. Something plastic comes flying out of the bag and when I pick it up, I recognize it as Janice's DVD, which I forgot to return to her the night of the lousy French dinner. It has a label with her address on it, somewhere in Venice, which isn't very far away but is not exactly on my route home, either. But what the hey, maybe she really needs it and I should swing by and drop it off. If she's not around, I can take some photos of the beach freaks.

The address is right on the beach, so after having to park friggin' miles away, I do get a chance to take photos of all the crazy and colorful street performers, hippie venders, half-naked roller bladders, crazy-ass jugglers and awe-struck tourists. As I'm clicking away I suddenly ask myself, why I'm even taking these photos in the first place? It's all very aimless and what exactly separates me from every other tourist who's doing the exact same thing? I guess I just don't know what I'm doing anymore, professionally or personally. I haven't even been calling around looking for work for like, two weeks now.

When I get to the address on the DVD, there's a group of some cool college kids hanging out on the patio. "I'm looking for Janice," I say to one of the kids.

"You wanna buy?" he asks.

"Buy what?" I ask in response. Are these kids selling drugs?

"Never mind," the kid says, losing immediate interest in me. "Janice is upstairs."

I take that as an invitation to enter the house and climb the badly in need of cleaning, stairs. When I get to the top of the stairs, through an open door, I can see Janice hanging out with a female friend. They're both drinking beers and dressed in skimpy beach clothes.

"Martin?" Janice says with obvious surprise.

"Hi," I say as coolly as I think Philip Marlowe would say it, climbing up the stairs of a broad's house as if it were the most normal thing in the world.

"This is, like, so weird. We were just talking about you. Come on in."

"You were just talking about me now? That is weird."

"No, not just now, now. A couple of days ago."

When I enter her room, she greets me with a light kiss on the lips which I think is very weird except that maybe that's the way they do things around here with all the cool, hip, free love aura that they've got going on in the place. The house is probably a free wheelin', free lovin' commune, like they had in the sixties. I have been noticing that this generation coming up is like a reincarnation of the sixties groovers, complete with their tie-dyed shirts and the long flowing floral dresses and the whole, 'I love you, man, it's all good,' hippie thing going on.

"What are you doing here? How did you get my..." I hold up her DVD and that answers all her questions. "Oh, my short. You're so sweet to bring it over. This is Jane, one of my roommates." I shake Jane's hand and now recognize her as the other woman of the threesome in the short. I'm half expecting the husband character to show up but, knowing how sensitive she is about her movie, I don't dare say anything.

"You look, like, so overdressed. Want something to drink?" asks Janice.

"Sure," I say, unbuttoning some shirt buttons. "Whatever you girls are having is fine."

Jane excuses herself and says that she's going to see what the guys are up to. "Keep them down there for about an hour, okay?" says Janice. "Tell them I have a client."

"A client?" I ask, when Jane leaves.

"I make jewelry. Want to see?"

"Sure," I say and just like before, she takes my hand in hers and leads me into what looks like her bedroom. Around the walls are display cases filled with handmade jewelry, earrings and bracelets mostly. "These are great," I say, even though I have no idea if they are or not, I have no eye for women's jewelry at all. "Is this, like, a tattoo portfolio?" I ask.

"Yeah, I do hemp tattoos."

"These are cool," I say and this time I mean it. The designs are really intricate and artistic.

"Do you want one?"

"How do you mean?"

"They're temporary, they come off in about a week or ten days. Let me give you one, it would look so good on you."

"Really?"

"Totally. You would look so cool with a tattoo. Pick one out and I'll go get us some beers." I've always like the Celtic knots with the interlacing of lines and spirals that look so delicate and yet strong, at the same time.

"What about this one?" I say, when she returns.

"That's one of my favorites," she says, almost with glee. "You need to take off your shirt." When I hesitate, she adds, "that's a Celtic breastplate, it goes on the chest. It's going to look so awesome on you, so...masculine. You're going to love it, you'll see."

"Okay."

"Take off your shirt and lie on the bed. I'll get the brushes."

So I take off my shirt and lie on her bed and although part of me is thinking that this is a bit weird, another part of me is telling me to relax, that this is where she does business with her clients and I shouldn't be so uptight and should instead consider it as getting to know my girlfriend's daughter, if she still is my girlfriend and to play by her rules, even if they are a little loosey-goosey for my liking. Maybe I am too controlled and conservative, just like the man.

"I've had people's personalities change after getting one of these," Janice says as she starts painting on my chest. I was not prepared for how intimate and sensual this whole tattoo thing was to become. It's hot in here and now that she's so close, I can feel her breath on my chest and, please god, stop my eyes from gravitating to her half-naked chest, even if she does have perfectly shaped breasts that are so pert and firm, they almost point upward. The soft and delicate brush strokes on my chest are so sensually arousing, I'm starting to get a hard on.

"The feel of the paint on the skin can be very erotic," Janice says, as if she's reading my mind. "Happens all the time, don't worry about it."

I'm not sure what exactly she's referring to but there's no way that I'm asking her to clarify. Can she tell I'm getting a boner? "How long does this usually take?" I ask, forcing my gaze onto some minor discoloration on the ceiling.

"I bet your fantasy is to have me and my mom at the same time."

"Excuse me?" I ask, as shocked, insulted and as astounded as I can possibly make myself sound without making it appear like I am faking it.

"Oh, come on. Sex is all you guys think about, admit it."

"I'm not…"

"A guy thinks about sex every seven seconds. That's a proven fact."

"Not this guy, trust me."

"You haven't once considered a threesome with you, me and my mom?"

"No. That's disgusting."

"How about with just you and me, then? You haven't considered that, either?"

"Of course not."

"Then why are you getting a boner?"

"Guys get boners all the time. It's out of our control. I hitched a ride from an old bearded trucker once and after a few miles of driving I got a boner. The guy looked like he escaped from ZZ Top and, no, I didn't want to sleep with him, either."

"What's ZZ Top?" Janice asks and casually takes off her shirt, exposing her very insufficient, delicately embroidered, lacy bra. I have a hard time telling the puzzle center of my brain to shift its focus away from trying to figure out if we can really see her nipples through the embroidery or if indeed, those darker areas are extra lace or simply the design of the bra itself.

"I should get going," I say and expect her to clear a way for me.

"If you didn't come here to have sex with me, then why did you come?"

"I came to return the DVD."

"Why didn't you mail it? Or give it to my mom? You didn't even call first. Afraid I would have turned you down?"

"I was in the neighborhood."

"You're such a guy, Martin. You're all a bunch of phonies."

Janice finally gets up and puts back on her shirt. I jump up off the bed and wrestle with my shirt to get the sleeves both going the right way.

"You know how many guys have fucked over my mom? I've lost count and you know what? She deserves better." As Janice slams the door on her way out, I take a look at the tattoo on my chest. Turns out that it's not a Celtic knot, after all, and it certainly doesn't look cool or masculine. In very crude calligraphy it says but two words: Hello mom.

"Oh, shit," I say out loud.

14. WHAT INFINITY FEELS LIKE

As I take a slow meandering stroll on the beach, I have this nagging feeling that something isn't quite right with me. I don't know what it is but there's something inside me that's not very healthy, almost as if there's some part of me that doesn't want me to be happy and when I get even a sniff of possible happiness, whatever it is wants no part of it and does its best to sabotage the whole deal.

Why did I drive down here to visit Frances' daughter? Janice is right, it wasn't about the DVD, I could have mailed it or given it to her mom. What was I thinking? Thinking back to that moment in the car, when I made the decision, I guess I was in kind of a weird place. I was feeling angry and maybe a bit rejected: did I want to strike back at Frances or get even with her in some way? If Janice wasn't so amazingly hot, would I have even wanted to drive down here? Did I want Janice to like me or think me cute? If so, would I have ditched Frances for her daughter?

Sometimes I hate being a guy and I hate to admit it but a lot of times guys do think with their penises and not with their heads. Jeez, would I have slept with Janice if she came on to me and seduced me? As nasty as it sounds, I wouldn't rule it out as a possibility. I would have been sorry afterwards, maybe even devastated and it would probably be something that I would never be able to forgive myself for, but I could see myself doing it, if the circumstances went that way, which thankfully, they did not.

I think that maybe, Janice is my fantasy woman that I've always wanted to date. She's young, gorgeous, a perfect 10 body and her intelligence level is not too dull to be a bore and not so bright that I can't easily handle her. She might have that angry feminist thing going on, but most likely that's a phase she's going through and I could just agree with everything she says until she left college and grew up a little.

Frances is so friggin' complicated and unpredictable that I really don't know if I'm up to the task. She talks and acts like she's wise and in control but then she does or says something that's utterly ridiculous and she comes across as some immature, wounded scaredy cat. I don't get her at all. I mean if she really has all her shit together, why is she alone at her age, married twice and her whole past such a screw up?

Then again, in some strange way, I do get her. She's like no one I've never met before, exotic, yet familiar, all at the same time. I feel so comfortable with her and so understood, like I've never felt with any other woman before, as if, on some level, we're great friends and compatriots that have known each other through many, many lifetimes. Or maybe I've just described how I feel about my mom. Do I have a mommy complex?

Ughhh, it's mind-numbingly complicated and maybe I should just go back to being alone where I'm not struggling with all this relationship stuff that I'm never, ever going to figure out or successfully get my head around.

I should go back to her place and break it off, face to face. It shouldn't come as any huge shock to her and considering whatever shit she was talking about when I told her that I loved her, it will probably be a massive relief to her too. At least I'll give her the decency of telling her in person and not in an email or text like I've heard this younger generation is known to do. Besides, Janice has probably been on the phone to her, telling her that I suggested we all have a threesome and that she should dump my sorry ass. It's a mess.

On the drive over, I mentally rehearse what I'm going to say: Frances, we're not right for each other. You need someone that's into Zen and yoga and I'm better off with someone a bit more naïve that drinks beer like a guy, swears and eats red meat. Someone a bit more like your daughter, maybe.

I shouldn't mention her daughter, that's just, euw.

Frances, it's been a wild ride and we had some fun times together but let's get off this crazy merry-go-round relationship thing before someone gets hurt. I think we could be good friends, no, I think we could be great friends, so what do you say, partner? That sounds like how Spencer Tracy broke it off with Katherine Hepburn in a few of their comedies. I should rewatch some of those, they were funny.

Frances, you're too old for me. I've learnt some great things from you and I'll be forever grateful but you've been around the block one too many times and at this point have too many miles on the clock for me to realistically consider any kind of future together. Eek, do I really think like this or am I channeling Mike? She wants…no, she *deserves* honest communication.

Frances, I'm too young for you. I've only had one serious relationship in my life where I can honestly say that I was in love, whereas, you have had many, so maybe we're just not evenly matched and to be perfectly honest, I don't know what you're talking about most of the time. Okay, that's the one. I'll lead with this and see where it takes us.

By the time I drive over there, eventually find parking and walk the six blocks to her place, I'm totally over it. In my head I've made peace with being alone and I'm already looking forward to getting back into my single life and my familiar routine of work, walks in the park, a few beers now and then with Mike and Gloria and maybe post newer stuff on my FaceBook page, which I've been seriously neglecting.

When Frances opens her door, the look of relief and total joy on her face takes me completely by surprise. She instantly hugs me and squeezes me so tightly that I have a hard time breathing. Without releasing her embrace, she shuts the door with her foot and somehow lets me know that she wants us to hug a little while longer without either of us breaking off or even speaking.

She's so warm and soft and smells of flowers that I'm lulled into a mental state of repose and all I want to do is close my eyes and stay exactly where I am. When I do close my eyes, I get the weirdest feeling. I could so totally fool my body into thinking that instead of standing upright, I'm actually stretched out, relaxing in a nice hot bath. Because that's exactly what hugging Frances feels like. It's trippy.

By the time her grip relaxes, I'm feeling relaxed and I'm aware that this is one of the most amazing hugs I've ever experienced. Before Frances, I've never thought much about the hug, probably because I haven't met anyone that was so into it the way that she is. But lately, I've grown to really like hugging and appreciate more its place in the pantheon of meaningful touch between two people.

When I hug Frances, or rather, when Frances hugs me and I hug her back, it's as if all the worries of the day and of the mind simply float away and return to the ethers from whence they came. Nothing else seems to matter except holding her tightly, right here and right now and sometimes it's actually hard to break off and feel that separation again. Holding her like this is so comforting and satisfying that it's like I've come home…it just feels like home.

"I'm so glad you came back," she says sweetly, without loosening her hold.

"Me too," I say and as if I've just experienced some kind of ninja mind-wipe, all the stuff that I've been thinking and rehearsing just evaporates from my brain and leaves a sense of peace and calm in its place.

"I love you too," she says and I'm so caught off guard and so unprepared, that a tear forms in my left eye and runs itchily down my cheek.

When she does break away from our hug, she does so very slowly and runs her hand down my arm to take hold of my hand. She looks into my eyes, which are now unashamedly teary and, with the most soulful look I've ever seen in anyone else's eyes, she says, "Come lie down and hold me."

Leading me to her bedroom, still without breaking contact, she moves her body into mine on the bed so that I'm spooning her and, as if our bodies had no weight, it is like we float on the bed and merge into each other, her into me and me into her, so much so that I didn't know where I end and she begins or where she ends and I begin.

It is the most surreal and most sublime feeling that I've ever had in my life and maybe similar to that one night where Mike and I smoked too much pot and in one brief flash of a moment, I experienced what infinity must feel like.

Then we both fall asleep.

When I wake back up, the room is in semi-darkness and Frances's face is lying against her pillow, facing me. As my eyes adjust, I can see that, if she was awake already, she has been watching me sleep. "Have you been watching me sleep?" I ask with a smile. No one has ever watched me sleep before.

"You're so well-behaved when you sleep," she says, playfully. She kisses me tenderly and I hold her face with my free hand and then softly stroke her cheek. One by one, she slowly and sexily opens the buttons on my shirt, which totally arouses me.

"What's that?" she asks as she peels back the left side of my shirt.

"What's what?" I ask, before I suddenly and shockingly remember.

"It looks like you have some kind of rash on your chest," she says, squinting in the half light to get a better look.

"Oh, that, no, it's not a rash, I was going to tell you…"

"Tell me what?"

"I dropped by Janice's place on my way home."

"Janice lives in Venice? That's not on your way home."

"I wanted to return her DVD which was in my bag all

the time and I...she told me to take care of it for her, that night, and I forgot and I figured she needed it and I was going to Venice anyway, to take some photos for a project I'm working on and anyway..."

Looking more than a little alarmed, Frances gets out of bed, zips up her jeans, buttons up her blouse and acts like she doesn't want to hear any more. It's as if her mind is made up, even though I haven't told her what happened and she wants me out of there, pronto.

"Nothing happened," I say, not knowing what to say. "She said that she does these tattoos and she insisted that she give me one, so I..."

Frances leaves the bedroom and I honestly feel like a turd, whatever that feels like and I really just want to bolt out the front door and run away at full speed down the street rather than have the conversation that I need to have with Frances if this relationship has any chance of survival.

Frances is in the kitchen making coffee when I sheepishly approach. "I don't want to hear any more," she says. "You should leave."

"I don't want to leave," I say, summoning all my bravery, "I want to talk this out."

"There is really nothing to talk about, Martin. Please go."

"Frances, nothing happened between us. Can't we even discuss it?" I interpret her silence to mean that she really doesn't want to talk and regretfully, at this moment can't stand the sight of me, either. I almost turn to leave and, based on my track record to date, I normally would have been long gone but something inside me, some stubborn, principled part of me is saying that this is a defining moment in my life, and to turn heel and run could be so damaging that I'd regret it for the rest of my life.

"Frances," I say softly, "if I have learned anything from you it's that honest communication is paramount to having any kind of relationship, with anybody. I know you feel like you hate me or despise me at this moment and I can understand that but if I walk out that door, then there's probably no way we can come back from this. You said you wanted a conscious relationship with true and honest communication? Well, here it is. Or do you only want it when it's on your terms?"

"You crossed a line, Martin."

"Can you stop doing what you're doing and we can sit down and talk?"

"Fine," says Frances, as she throws a dish cloth across the counter top.

I sit down on the sofa as an invitation for her to join me. She does, although she sits away from me at the far end. I slowly and carefully tell her the story, beginning with finding the DVD in my car and ending with discovering that the Celtic knot tattoo was, in fact, something else. I talk about how I wasn't really sure what it all meant or what was going through Janice's mind, nor what she had hoped to achieve by her devious bait and switch. I finish the tale by somberly opening my shirt and revealing the tattoo for Frances to fully experience for herself: Hello mom.

"I honestly don't know if she was protecting you from another sex-crazed boyfriend or trying to get one over on you by bragging that she could have stolen a boyfriend from you, I don't know."

"Could she?" asks Frances. "Could she have stolen a boyfriend from me?"

"Of course not."

"She is going through some weird phase, lately."

"How do you mean?"

"All this feminist stuff, she was never like that before. It's probably a mix of whatever feminist courses she's doing in college and a belated adolescence where she seems to blame me for all her childhood instability, not having a father…" As Frances becomes tearful, part of me heaves a sigh of relief that the intense pressure that was on me now seems to be off. I'm not sure if I should come closer and hold her but, rather than risk another rejection, or have the focus switch back to me, I stay put.

"She actually told me that I ruined her entire childhood." Frances can't hold back her tears and I do move closer to embrace her, which she actually welcomes. She sobs in my arms.

15. THE COLUMBUS EFFECT

I sleep over with Frances but for the first night since we've been together, it isn't sexy. In fact, I would describe our togetherness as downright cold and I barely sleep at all. Feeling very fragile and vulnerable, Frances asks me to stay but she seems to have withdrawn into herself. I feel like I'm superfluous to whatever it is that she's going through and maybe would have been better off going home. It's fierce awkward and I have no idea how to be with her or what to say to her when she's being so distant like this.

"We should get ready for the seminar," she says and then I remember that it starts today and then I wonder: she now wants to go to a relationship seminar? Seriously?

"You still want to go?" I ask gently.

"You don't?"

"No, I do. I just wasn't sure if…sure, let's go."

I feel like now I'm walking on eggshells around her and I've no idea how to make things better between us. Does she just need some time? What is she thinking? Is she thinking about her daughter or me or her past failed relationships, what?

"Would you like me to drive?" I ask, when we get to her car.

"No, I'm fine," she says, without looking at me.

As we drive in silence I'm now wishing that I was somewhere else, anywhere else, besides going to some ludicrous relationship seminar with a woman that's acting at best, like she doesn't care about me and at worst, like she hates my guts.

If I was with Mike, and he was acting like this, I'd punch him on the shoulder and say, 'snap out of it, man, you're depressing as fuck, let's go grab a beer,' and invariably he'd smile and say, 'you're right, dude, I'm feeling like crap today, let's go get shit-faced,' and off we'd go to the nearest bar and pretty much stay till closing. And that would be it, end of weirdness. You can't do that with a woman. This silent shit sucks.

We sit in a small function room of a hotel along with maybe twenty other couples and one strange guy on his own who probably misread the brochure that said it was for couples and not for single guys hoping to get coupled up. Dr. Redmond Clark is first up and he's going to give a PowerPoint presentation about something called the Columbus Effect and other fascinating oddities.

Dr. Clark is a total geek that seems to think in his head that he's cool, which makes him come off looking ten times geekier. He cracks some lame jokes, presumably to get everyone to like him and maybe it's his way of saying, hey I know I have a bunch of letters after my name but I'm a really cool guy and fun to have a beer with, too. Then he dims the lights and starts his presentation and in an instant he becomes deathly serious. I look at Frances and smile, as if to say, 'can you believe this guy?' but she doesn't smile back. Not good.

"One of the first questions I like to ask couples is, 'why are you in relationship in the first place?' Some people answer that question by saying: because it's fun or I like the way she/he looks or I want someone to do stuff with, I don't want to be alone...'

"These are all valid answers but the one true, overriding answer is that the biology of evolution has hardwired you that way. The concern of evolution is not that you have someone to go to the movies with or to ensure that you have a dance partner, no. The concern of evolution is the continuance of the species. It's the evolutionary impulse that is largely responsible for mate selection among animals. Humans, despite whether we might like to think otherwise, are no exception to that impulse."

Already bored, I look to Frances to see what kind of response a neutral smile will get me but she doesn't shift her gaze from the PowerPoint slide of a bunch of words under the title, "Evolutionary Imperatives." I look around the room to see who else thinks this is a load of you-know-what but not only are most people sitting forward in their seats, some of them are taking notes.

I'd hate to be the only one here that feels like heckling but either the guys are really into it or they're doing a good job of faking interest to keep their girlfriend's happy. For the sake of the evolutionary imperative of the camaraderie of guyhood, I'm hoping it's the latter.

"Let's look what happens when two people, 'fall in love,' shall we? First of all, the body releases an extremely potent chemical cocktail called phenylethylamine or PEA for short. This love soup provides the body with a natural high: colors seem brighter, the world seems friendlier and so on. Monkeys injected with PEA demonstrate hyper sexuality and "moonstruck" behavior with their companion. If their companion is removed, the monkey will experience immediate withdrawal symptoms or what we might call 'love sickness.' An amazing facet of this drug cocktail is that the drug only works in the presence of the other lover, the object of one's affection, you might say.

"After two to four years, the body ceases production of PEA. Nature has done its work, perhaps hoping that within this period one or more offspring have been produced and after which it is now up to the couple to either stay together or leave."

I kind of mentally doze off with my eyes open while Dr. Coolgeek drones on and almost puts me to sleep. I rouse myself now and then to catch a few words and, in the midst of intense boredom, I notice a really cool thing. If I tune out and don't pay attention to any words in particular but just let them all blend into each other, like that chant music that some yoga people listen to, I notice that my mind will 'wake up' to some specific words that get my attention, without my conscious mind having any control over it.

Sex...intercourse...copulation...sexual...anal...conjuga tion. Maybe guys do have a one-track mind, after all. But then again, I am listening to a lecture on sex or evolution or some combination thereof. Then he shows a video showing two rats in a cage and that gets my attention.

"Let's talk about sex, shall we?' he continues with a knowing smirk. "If you put a male and a female rat together in a cage, they will be observed to initially copulate at a high rate of repetition." I hear some nervous laughs from people but then again, watching two rats going at it over and over again, it is kind of funny.

"As the honeymoon period comes to an end, the rate of copulation declines considerably. Familiarity tends to lead to a lack of sexual interest." The rats are now slowing down until finally they stop and one of the rats, I guess the male, gets bored and goes off sniffing for food or something. Then they replace one of the rats with another rat and it's off to the races all over again.

"If the female is removed and replaced by another, the male miraculously becomes rejuvenated and the rate of copulation is immediately restored to earlier, higher levels." Okay, this is funny. "Scientists have called this the Columbus Effect. The same behavior is observed with monkeys and yes, you guessed it, humans. Sexual boredom is one of the strongest factors operating against stable relationships in both the human and animal kingdom. When sex between a couple comes to a halt, a break up in the relationship is sure to follow."

I can hear some uncontrolled groans and some sighing by some women in the audience, like they just discovered why all their boyfriends have been cheating on them since forever. I'm making a note to remember this and maybe Google it when I get home. I can see how this could be a darn good defense to use when confronted about cheating, not that I ever would: 'you don't understand, honey, don't blame me, I couldn't help it, it's the Columbus Effect.'

"In the absence of social restrictions, the human male would be promiscuous throughout the whole of his life. Women, however, tend to be more monogamous. Women want a lot of sex with the man they love; men want to have a lot of sex with a lot of different women."

Wow, for me, this explains a lot. I'm not going to beat myself up over wanting to…

Without warning, Frances is up out of her chair and heading for the exit at some speed. I jump up and follow her. Catching up with her outside, I have to call her name to stop her speed walking. "I can't do this," she says.

"No, I'm glad," I say relieved that we're out of there and we don't have to return for two more days of torture. "Me, neither. That thing sucked."

"I don't mean that," she says. "I mean us. I can't do this… I can't do us. I'm sorry." She turns and races off toward the car. I hurry around to her and head her off.

"That's it?" I ask. "After all the talk about issues and honest communication and stuff: you're just going to walk?"

"I can't do this anymore."

"Why don't you say that you're scared? I'm scared. Maybe everybody's scared when they get close to commitment and intimacy but won't admit it. I'll admit it. I'm scared. I got so scared I almost screwed it up. Maybe I did screw it up. Did I screw it up?"

"I don't know, Martin. I need to leave."

I stand there in a kind of shock as I can feel my brain trying to figure it all out. Yesterday, I was ready to walk but Frances was really nice to me and I changed my mind. Now she's ready to walk and I've no idea what to say or do to make her change her mind.

This is so peculiar. Boy meets girl and now boy is about to lose girl. What would Tom Hanks say to Meg Ryan at this point in the movie? I take Frances' hands in mine and look her straight and meaningfully in the eyes.

"Frances. You're a beautiful, caring, wonderful woman and…" This is always the best speech of the movie that's so heartfelt and incredibly well written, that it brings a tear to the audience's eye. I try my best to remember what Billy Crystal said to Meg Ryan in *When Harry Met Sally*, but I'm drawing a blank and I have to say something or she's going to walk…"I'm really sorry you can't follow your own advice," I finally blurt out.

I knew it was really lame even as I was saying it and Frances does not look at all on the verge of tears and even less likely to have a change of heart. I stand aside and without a parting word and finally, with some tears in her eyes, Frances walks past me and out of my life.

It takes me two buses and a good stretch of walking to get back to my apartment. It feels like forever since I actually spent a night in my own bed and at this point, I am really looking forward to it.

First thing that hits me when I get through the front door is the weird smell. The air smells rank, like sweaty socks. The place is a mess with take out and pizza boxes, empty beer bottles and half empty bottles of hard liquor all over the place. I can pretty much tell by the placement and the general assortment of the take out boxes that this wreckage is not from a party the night before: this took some time to end up in this kind of a neglected state.

When I get to the hallway I see Mike sitting on the floor of the bathroom. The door is open and he's still wearing his boxers and a tee shirt from when he got up this morning, or judging by his unshaven looks, this afternoon. He looks dazed and holds a beer in his hand that he doesn't even seem aware of.

"What's going on, Mike? You look like shit. You okay?"

"She left me, Marty. Gloria dumped my sorry ass. Can you believe it?"

"No, I can't believe it. You were the best thing that ever happened to her."

"She met…was seeing someone else, I don't know the details."

"Where did she get the time to meet someone else? She practically lived here, rent free, but that's not important."

"I think it was this guy we met at this party. I went to the bathroom, there was a long line…and when I get back she's talking to this guy, a fucking photographer, can you believe it? Told her he could get her into modeling. I guess he got into her pants instead."

"Jeez, she fell for the old, 'get you into modeling' line. The number of times I've used that line and it never once paid off." He doesn't react to what I just said, almost like he didn't hear me, which I'm thankful for because now and again I totally shock myself at how insensitive I can be at times. Sometimes, I may be a little bit too much obsessed about me, I've noticed.

"I should have known better. Never bring your chick to a party, man," Mike says, deeply obsessed with his own thoughts, I'd imagine.

"I know, I know," I say as I pat him consolingly on the shoulder.

So, I grab two six packs of beers from the fridge and sit down on the bathroom floor with my buddy, our backs resting against the bathtub. We barely much say anything to each other; we both feel like shit, what is there to say? Simply by sitting side-by-side on the hard linoleum floor, with our unspoken tacit agreement that love sucks, we support and console each other. We don't move till we finish every beer in the house.

16. THE WEDDING

I'm walking through my favorite park in Santa Monica, pretty much back where I started except I'd like to think a tad bit older and wiser. It's almost sunset and the happy and in-love couples are out in force, some strolling arm in arm, some standing by the railing, watching the ocean, some are picnicking and some are kissing. I'm not taking their photographs anymore; I've put that project to bed. Instead what I'm inclined to take lately is the sunset itself.

Every night it's different and every picture I take seems to reveal something marvelous within the texture of color and hue of the sky and the sun and sometimes some clouds. Since I've started this project, I've since discovered that there's no such thing as an ordinary sunset or a generic sunset. Just like snowflakes, no two sunsets are exactly alike.

Two things have really surprised me since this whole Frances thing. First, it's been really hard to stop myself from contacting her and second, for as little time as I've known her, I never thought I'd miss anyone as much as I miss her.

Sometimes I think that maybe I'm just in love with the idea of being in love. I do love sunsets and romance and the sweetness of touch and the rush of sexual…copulation, for want of a better word. I don't think I've had a relationship that has lasted longer than the romance and maybe that's all it is and will be for me. How can I move on and get past that? I think that I would have stuck it out with Frances but she kind of blind-sided me by being the first one to bow out.

"Mind if I sit here?" I turn and see that a really hot girl is asking to share the bench.

"No, not at all," I say and remind myself that they say that the time you meet that someone special is when you're not looking, when you're not at all trying.

"Is this the most romantic spot on earth, or what?" the young woman comments.

"It sure is," I say and I'm aware that I'm sounding world weary and wise for my age. Funny thing is, as beautiful as this young woman is, I have no interest in hitting on her. Zilch. I was joking before about being imprinted on Frances but I'm not so sure that it's a joke anymore. Or maybe I'm just in love with the pining, the longing for this woman that I connected so deeply with; which is part and parcel of the whole romance thing that I have been obsessing about, right? Heck if I know.

A young man approaches and the young woman springs up and they kiss solidly on the lips. I could have bet money that she was hitting on me. It's like my whole dating radar is busted or maybe it's coming across that I don't give a damn about the whole dating scene anymore. Roxanne is getting married on Sunday and the whole thing about bringing or not bringing a hot babe to the party? I don't give a shit.

Just to further emphasize how little I care about whom I show up to the wedding with, I decide that Mike is going to be my plus one. Mike and Roxanne hated each other and if hate is too strong a word, then let's just say that they couldn't stand the sight of each other, pretty much the way I used to feel about Gloria.

I'm well aware that Mike is in no shape to be going anywhere, let alone a fancy wedding but he's my best friend and we've stuck with each other through thick and thin and if it came to it, we'd probably take a bullet for each other, it doesn't get tighter than that.

"I think I'm gonna hurl," Mike says as he takes a major gulp out of his hip flask. I haven't seen him eating in days and even though he's dressed in a jacket and a nice pair of jeans, with his hair unkempt and his scruffy excuse for a beard, he still looks like he just rolled out of a garbage dumpster.

"If you're seriously going to throw up, let me know

quick so I can pull over, okay? I just got the car cleaned."

"Why? You think you're going to get lucky? You think Roxanne is going to change her mind at the last minute and run into your arms begging you to take her for one last ride in your piece of shit, ten year old car?"

"Could happen," I say, playing along. "She'd have to beg real hard, though. Once I dump 'em, I don't take 'em back." We both laugh and even if he is in bad shape I'm glad that we're going together.

"You need to pull over."

"Seriously?"

Before I even get to the turn signal, Mike spews vomit all over the dashboard.

Our clean up detour means that we didn't make it on time for the ceremony so we go straight to the wedding reception. As we enter the hotel, Mike peels off to go find the nearest restroom so he can get himself cleaned up.

"Martin!" Roxanne declares as I get to the sign in table. Standing with some of the bridesmaids and welcoming the guests, she looks truly radiant.

"Congratulations, Roxanne. You look amazing."

"Thank you, Martin. So do you. Did you come by yourself?"

"No. Mike had to go to the restroom. You remember Mike, right?"

"You brought your roommate?" Roxanne asks with a mix of surprise and pity. "Yes, of course I remember Mike. How is he?"

"Here he comes, you can ask him, yourself."

Roxanne watches a puke and water-stained, disheveled Mike walk unsteadily down the hall, as someone might watch a runaway train approach an end of the line train station, with a mix of awe and terror, perhaps.

"Roxanne, you old witch, you look amazing," says Mike, going in for a cheek kiss. Roxanne quickly turns away to greet another arriving couple with an over-the-top greeting.

"You dodged a bullet, my friend," says Mike. "Now let's go drink all their free booze."

We park ourselves at an outlying table away from the central action and proceed to drink all the beer we can carry back to the table without looking like a disgraceful pair of alcoholics.

"I don't even know what I'm doing here," I say to Mike. "What are we doing here?"

"You're here, my friend, to stick it to her. You're here to show her how amazing you are so that she eats her heart out."

"Oh, yeah. I forgot."

"And the free booze."

Mike gets up but misjudges his step and almost keels over, taking the tablecloth with everything on it with him. "Relax," I tell him. "I'll get the drinks. And you *will* pay for the car detail."

"Of course, I will," says Mike. "Just go get some more refreshments."

Since things ended with Frances, I've had several incidents on the street where I thought I saw her. On each occasion, the woman would turn around or walk closer to me and I would realize that, while in some way they resembled Frances, they obviously weren't her.

As I head for the refreshments, a woman with her back to me, by the punch bowl, is another dead ringer for Frances. I've only seen such a thing in movies and I thought it was only some kind of movie convention, sort of like so we know what the lead character is thinking: he's missing the girl. But it seems to be an actual condition: I am missing Frances. When the woman turns around, she looks to her left and then straight ahead and sees me. To my shock and amazement, it *is* Frances. She is radiant and dressed in an outrageously sexy dress. She looks absolutely, hands down…stunning.

"Frances?" I say, with obvious puzzlement. "What are you doing here?"

"I thought you were a no-show," she says, with a mix of relief and excitement.

"What? No, I mean, we missed the ceremony but...what are you doing here?"

"*We* missed the ceremony? Did you bring somebody?" she asks, looking around.

"Yeah. I brought my roommate, Mike. The sorry looking dude sitting by himself over by the kid's table."

"He's not looking too good."

"His girlfriend broke up with him and I guess he's experiencing PEA withdrawal."

Frances thinks about that one for a second and then smiles with recognition. "What about you?" she asks. "Any PEA withdrawal symptoms you'd like to share?"

"Maybe later. What I would like to know is what you're doing here. Not that I'm not pleased to see you, I am. Very much so."

"I'm here because you invited me. I said, yes, that no matter what happens with us, I will go with you, remember? I may be a scaredy cat when it comes to relationships, but when it comes to attending other people's weddings...I'm pretty much good to my word."

"Are you alone?"

"Of course. I almost went home after the ceremony but I decided, what the heck, maybe I'll meet someone special at the reception." She smiles that amazingly beautiful smile at me and adds: "And I was right."

"What now?" I stand and stare, unable to function much beyond drinking in her beauty.

"Well, I think we should stick to the plan, don't you?"

"What plan?"

"We dance and cavort and frolic in front of the bride and all of the time I won't be able to keep my roving hands off of you."

"That sounds like a good plan to me." All I want to do is hug her and squeeze her and smell her and taste her…

"Showing up with sadsack over there, she already thinks you're a loser, right?"

"Oh, yeah," I say, giving a wave to Mike.

"We'll show her, then."

Then Frances grabs my hand and leads me to the dance floor where we dance what can only be described as our version of the forbidden dance: suggestive verging on vulgar. Her sense of fun is back and I love her. Yes, I do love her. With her Jennifer Grey to my Patrick Swayze, we dirty dance up and down the modestly-sized dance floor. We do manage to get Roxanne's attention and I couldn't care less what kind of looks she is throwing our way, I only have eyes for Frances.

I have no idea where this woman is at in her head or what she's been thinking since we last parted, and there's no way I'm going to risk having a serious discussion about relationship or feelings or the future of 'us' or even PEA and Christopher Columbus, at least for tonight.

Zen and the art of honest communication will have their day but for now, fun Frances is back and she is one of my most favorite people in the entire world. I want to make her smile and laugh the way she makes me laugh and smile. Judging by the way everyone looks at us and smiles, I would say that whatever it is we've got going, other people can definitely see it and it's worth making the hard yards to keep it alive and grow it further.

I've never been much of a dancer but with Frances, we dance all night and I've never had so much fun. For some bizarre reason that continues to confound me, Mike, no matter what kind of state the guy is in, women…good-looking women *always* find him attractive. I can see that he is barely able to function as a passable human being and coming here, had zero interest in hooking up tonight but for some mind-boggling reason, one of the really cute bridesmaids took a shine to him and talked him into leaving behind all the free booze and going back to her place.

I'm happy for him but I also know that although this new chick is going to replace Gloria in his affections and take him out of his post-moonstruck depression, like all of us, it seems, he is merely repeating the cycle. Fall in love, get dumped, fall in love, get dumped...

Except that's not what I'm feeling with Frances, right now. In fact, I would go out on a limb and say that this really feels like it is the last relationship I'll ever have.

We're on her bed and she's somewhere beneath me and yet beside me...From memory, we're doing Tantric Sex position number two from the book and I'm doing everything in my power not to come but instead to hold it and circulate it and...obviously whatever pained expression is on my face is comical because she laughs and then I laugh and then her body relaxes and then my body relaxes...and I explode. Ooh, baby, baby, I love your way, I want to be with you night and day, ooh, baby, baby...I spontaneously break into yet another love song...

ABOUT THE AUTHOR

Dermot Davis is an award-winning playwright, having had plays performed in Dublin, Boston and Los Angeles. His creative work encompasses varied genres and styles — drama, comedy, and, more recently, sci-fi, with a special focus on human themes and characters transformed by life experience. A sometimes actor, he is a co-founder of the Laughing Gravy Theatre (which performed Irish Vaudeville and excerpts of Irish literary works as well as drama, including the original stage plays of Mr. Davis) where he and other members of the troupe were artists-in-residence at the Piccolo Spoleto Festival in Charleston, South Carolina. He currently resides in Los Angeles. Follow him on his Goodreads.com Author Page at http://www.goodreads.com/author/show/6565450.Dermot_Davis

24882547R00088

Made in the USA
Charleston, SC
08 December 2013